A NECESSARY END

SARAH PINBOROUGH
F. PAUL WILSON

A NECESSARY END

Shadowridge Press

A NECESSARY END

First trade edition published January 2014
by Shadowridge Press

This is a work of fiction. All characters,
organizations, and imagined events portrayed in
this novel are either products of the author's imagination
or are used fictitiously.

Cover illustration by Wayne Miller

A signed hardcover edition limited to
333 copies was published by Thunderstorm Books
in Novermber 2013

ISBN-978-0-9897796-1-6

www.shadowridgepress.com

Acknowledgments

Thanks to Mary Wilson, Steven Spruill,
Elizabeth Monteleone,
Jennifer Bowers, and Dannielle Romeo

for
Penn & Teller

Seeing that death, a necessary end,
Will come when it will come.

Julius Caesar – William Shakespeare

THURSDAY

NIGEL

"Do you really think that shit has any effect, or is it just for show to make us all feel better? I know where I'd put my money. Those insecticide companies are all laughing hard at our expense."

Nigel had barely noticed the man sitting beside him; he'd been too busy letting his sweat cool in the air-conditioning and enjoying the relief at having made it onto the plane. His AMEX card had taken the three-thousand-pound hit for the business-class seat with no chance in hell he could pay it back, but he'd worry about that when he got home. Maybe the data he had stored on his thumb drive would persuade Malcolm to part with the cash from the newspaper's accounts.

Still, he was on the plane and that was all that mattered. British Airways flights out of moribund Cairo were rare now and were taking only nationals. Even with the city nigh deserted, they had far more people waiting than seats. England was supposed to be safe and everyone wanted to go home. He'd been lucky.

"I mean," the man continued, "it's hardly a secret that it's gone worldwide."

Air stewards holding masks over their faces moved up and down the aisles spraying the air with insect repellent, the smell at once acrid and comforting. Nigel looked across at his fellow passenger. Shirt with wide wet patches circling low from his armpits. Hanging jowls. A nose red as much from booze as the Egyptian sun. *Twat* was the word that sprung immediately to mind.

The plane's engines thrummed louder and they jolted slightly as the pilot pushed them back off the stand.

"But then it's all their fault, isn't it?" The man leaned in conspiratorially across the divide, close enough for his tangy breath to assault Nigel's senses. "You know. The *blacks*."

"You think?" Nigel said, unable to stop himself despite not wanting to get drawn into five hours of inane conversation.

As soon as they were up, he intended to sleep. Hadn't had enough of it recently, and he found something reassuring about being thirty-six thousand feet in the air above the plague and its attendant madness.

"Of course." The jowls wobbled in affirmation. "Just like AIDS. All comes down to Africa. To the blacks." The man must have seen some flicker of amusement in Nigel's expression and his eyes hardened. "Only idiots think otherwise."

"Champagne, sir?" The air hostess smiled at them, breaking the moment.

Nigel took a glass. The whole world was descending into chaos but you still got champagne on take-off. Stiff upper lip and all that. Sometimes you just had to laugh. Or cry. Or simply wonder if anyone truly sane was left in the world.

As they pulled onto the main runway, he leaned back in his chair and peered out of the window at the shimmering heat on the tarmac. To the west, a huge plume of black smoke marred the cloudless sky. Cairo was burning. Again. But his mind was still on the man beside him, and those diminishing millions of others like him. Maybe he should add some of this hysteria to his article. Malcolm would like it. Race. When you can't blame anything else then blame the color of someone's skin.

"They say Paris was the fault of a white man," Nigel said after a long enough pause to allow the man beside him to get comfortable in his chair.

He kept his eyes on the endless blue sky that cut across the dusty desert horizon. Now that he was settled perhaps it was time to unsettle him.

"I beg your pardon?"

"He was Spanish. A Catholic of all things. God Squad terrorist. A crazy."

He turned back to the man. For a second he wondered what his name was and then realized that he didn't want to know. He couldn't imagine anything about this man he wanted to retain.

"You're lying."

"I'm a journalist, so that's always a possibility." Nigel kept his tone light and conversational. "But not this time. I could tell you how he snuck them in, got them past the sprays and border checks, but that would spoil the story for you when it comes out in the papers. But he was white and he said he was doing it for his *God*. And that" – this time it was his turn to lean forward a little – "was it for Paris."

He smiled and took a small amount of satisfaction in seeing the smug face beside him pale slightly.

"So maybe you're right. Maybe all the sprays and DDT planes are just to make us feel better. Because you can't stop the crazies." He took another sip of his champagne. "So if you want to blame anyone, why don't you look to the Almighty? Seems like everyone else is, one way or another."

The aircraft surged forward as it built toward take-off and Nigel leaned back in his seat and closed his eyes. Goodbye Cairo International Airport and thank you. Something told him the next five hours would be peaceful enough.

People could speak of God or color, but he was pretty sure he had the answer tucked into his pocket. They could all read it and weep when it went to press.

Abby would. What would she make of his story? After they'd finally got a connection last night and managed a ten-minute crackling chat, he'd actually been looking forward to getting home. She'd sounded like Abby – the Abby in his head – warm and sweet and healthy. Now the first twinges of dread were kicking in. The needles. The machines. And that fistula. His stomach lurched as the plane rose but he wasn't sure it was entirely due to the momentum.

He felt the familiar tightening in his shoulder muscles and tried to force it to let go.

More champagne, that was what he needed. More champagne and then five hours of peaceful rest high above the insanity that raged below.

NAVY OPENS FIRE ON AFRICAN FLOTILLA

GIBRALTAR – After warnings to turn around and return to their home ports were ignored by the countless small craft fleeing North Africa, the Royal Navy received orders to open fire. "Let them land in Spain or France," one officer was overheard. "They're not setting foot on British soil." (The Times of London)

ABBY

Abby stepped into the TARDIS-size vestibule of the Purr 'n Woof and closed the outer door behind her. She'd thought it was hot out on the pavement – unseasonably so for September – but this box was an oven. She did a slow turn, inspecting the stifling air around her.

A speaker in the upper right corner crackled. *"All clear?"*

"Looks good," she said.

A prolonged *buzzzz* and the inner door swung open. She yanked off the sunglasses and ski mask as she stepped into the air-conditioned interior.

"Oh Lord, this feels heavenly," she said.

The proprietor, known to her only as George, stepped from behind the counter. Skinny, pale, wild hair, thick glasses, wearing a faded yellow Hawaiian shirt aswarm with giant carp. He indicated the padded stool to her left.

"Just drop your things there. How is it?"

"Outside?" She pulled off her knit wool gloves and long raincoat. "Not bad. At least not as you can tell. Hot of course, but the few out and about are dressed for winter. Other than that, just another sunny summer day of rampant paranoia in London Town."

She saw a shadow flit across George's features and realized she'd just passed through a security vestibule into his pet shop.

Oh, Lord, what have I said?

"You, of course," she added quickly, "have something to protect – besides your health, I mean."

He nodded. "Well, yes, I suppose I do. It's not paranoia when they're really out to get you, right?" He laughed a little at his own joke – an irritating sound.

"And the more they migrate to London, the more I have to protect what I sell."

"It's bad, but they'll think of something."

He gave her a wary look. "Where'd you hear that? The telly? They only parrot what they're fed, and they're fed lies to keep us all from panicking. It's all going to hell out there."

"Just have faith," she said. "That's all you need." She wasn't entirely unaware of the conflict between that statement and her present location and she tried to ignore how much she disliked it. Her weakness.

With a noncommittal grunt he slipped back behind the counter. "I've got your order ready."

As George searched through an array of tiny boxes clustered to the side of the cash register, Abby glanced around. Purr 'n Woof... she tried to think of a worse name for a pet shop. Surely she could. Nope. Came up blank.

But she'd been buying her aquarium supplies here for years and had grown used to it. All the aquaria stood empty now, however. Well, not empty, not really. Silken strands had replaced fish-laced water.

What has he done with the fish? she wondered. Sushi?

A couple of dogs barked in the rear kennels. Well, at least they remained among the living. But if George were Korean...

Don't go there, Abby.

But really, if food supplies got as bad as predicted, who knew?

"Right," George said, picking out a box and holding it up. "Here we are."

He slid it toward her: an old ring box wrapped with fibrous tape.

She couldn't help smiling as she leaned closer. "Are you proposing? If so, I should let you know that I'm already—" The words dried up when she saw the price printed on the front. "Four hundred? We agreed on three."

He looked down and traced a design in the countertop with a finger. "Aside from the growing swarms in London, there's been no word out of Brighton all day."

Her flaring anger abruptly cooled.

"No word? What's that mean?"

He shrugged and looked up. "Just that. The council, the police, the fire brigade – nobody's responding."

Her chest tightened. "That's impossible. *Somebody's* there. *Somebody's* got a phone that works."

"That's what you'd think, wouldn't you. So that leads to one conclusion: They're all dead or dying."

"But that's impossible!"

"Really? That's where it started here."

"The Channel…"

They'd said the Channel was going to give protection… that the flies couldn't cross it.

"Water didn't stop it hopping from Tangier to Gibraltar, now did it? Not with nutcases helping it all along."

She'd heard rumors that Mungus had loosed whole containers of flies in Brighton, straight off a ferry. They took hold there and spread north like… well, like a plague.

"So fast?"

"Faster than they've been letting on. You haven't seen what's happening? Don't believe the TV or the radio or papers. Look around out there."

She shook her head. "I haven't been feeling well."

Too true. She was overdue for her dialysis. She'd been delaying it, trying to stretch her supplies, and she felt like crap.

"No matter what they say, the flies are already here in droves." He shook his head. "Anyway, the price is four hundred quid."

"Because Brighton's gone?"

"Yeah. And with the way things are going here, money's not going to be worth anything soon anyway, so—"

She managed not to shout. Just barely. "Then why do you want more of mine?"

"Because of what money can buy *now*. Not going to be much to buy later on."

She looked past him and for the first time noticed cartons of canned goods stacked against the rear wall. Hoarding. It didn't surprise her. If she was honest she had more tins than she needed in the cupboards at home. Shopping subconsciously in preparation?

"Well, I don't have four hundred on me."

"I told you cash–"

"You also told me three hundred!" *Now* she was shouting. She stepped closer. "I've been a customer here a long, long time, George, and you're pulling this bait-and-switch shite on me? What's happened to you?"

He flinched. "Okay, okay. Three."

She'd had the bills ready in her jeans pocket. She fished them out and pushed them across the counter, then held up the box.

"Now show me what I just bought."

"It's sealed for your own protection."

That caught her off guard. "*My* protection?"

He rolled his eyes. "If you lose the sac, I won't replace it.

"I'd hardly expect you to – not after trying to jack up the price."

"Now wait just a–"

"No waiting, George." She tapped the box. "Show me the merchandise."

He hesitated, then heaved a dramatic sigh, found a utility knife under the counter, and went about slitting the tape with surgical precision.

As Abby watched, it occurred to her that she might make a practice of holding off her dialysis before dealing with people. The malaise made her cranky and more assertive. Any other time she'd probably have been begging him to accept a check for the extra hundred quid, the dirty–

She squelched the thought. Be forgiving. That is the way.

With the tape cut, he popped the top. Instead of a ring, a small, fluffy ball, maybe half again as big as the head of a cotton swab, nestled on the satin lining. Not white, though. More of a beige.

"That's it then?"

"That's it." Pride tinged his tone. "*T. duellica*."

"Tea...?"

"*Tegenaria duellica*." He snapped the box shut. "Take it home, open it, place it on a plate somewhere out of the way but not in direct sunlight, and keep an eye on it. In no time you should have about fifty hatchlings."

"God willing," she said.

"And the best thing," he added, "no mum around to eat the little darlings."

She repressed a shudder. "Lovely."

She bundled up, pocketed the box, and let George buzz her through to the outdoors. She stepped out of the makeshift vestibule and stood blinking in the sunlight. The air felt the temperature of blood, and nearly as thick and moist. London went through this type of September every few years or so, but why did this have to be one?

God's will, she guessed.

She wondered about God's plan for her in all this. Nigel, of course, would say there was no plan – no God, in fact – but Abby knew better. She prayed Nigel would see the light. And soon.

She looked around. Where *was* everybody? Lunch hour on a Thursday in London and the streets were virtually deserted. The same at church this morning. She went to mass every day and had noticed a precipitous decline in attendance over the past week. Here on the pavement the few people out and about were mummied up like her except for a homeless fellow across the road wearing dirty shorts, a dirtier T-shirt, and tattered sneakers. He was pawing through a near-empty wastebasket. Slim pickings there.

She started walking, glancing through the window of a sandwich shop as she passed. Maybe four people at the tables, but the dreadlocked take-away delivery boy was loaded down as he exited. Made sense: Let someone else risk the plague for your lunch. But how much longer would their supplies last?

She shook her head. No one knew the number of plague cases in London. The news said it had been spotty so far, yet Twitter and Facebook and the blogosphere screamed cover-up as they posted lists of the sick people they knew. Certainly the hospital where she volunteered had its fill of cases. Whatever the truth, everyone had conceded the streets to it. The plague had already won.

She turned and headed for home.

THE NEW VAMPIRES

MIAMI – They only come out at night…
No, we're not referencing the old Edgar Winter Group, we're talking about the new nocturnal lifestyle that has taken hold in South Florida since the flies arrived in force. It's not a vogue, it's a necessity. The flies awaken and begin their incessant buzzing as soon as the sun clears the horizon, filling the air until after it sets. In the old days of South Beach, turning the diurnal clock on its head by sleeping all day and going out to do what needed to be done during the dark time might have been a lifestyle choice. Now it has become a simple matter of self-preservation. (Rolling Stone Daily)

ABBY

In the old days she'd have got off the tube at Angel and strolled the length of Upper Street, enjoying the buzz of the cafes and shops filled with a heady mixture of successful creative types who could afford to spend their weekday lunch times sipping coffee or wine at the many bistros and restaurants that were never short of clientele. Now, however, the pavements were empty and the boarded-up shops and eateries simply served to depress her, but she refused to let that stop her from the walk.

Three or four cafes still tried valiantly to maintain normalcy in all the hysteria, and she would always buy at least a coffee in one of them every time she came this way. Sometimes she didn't even drink it, but would wander farther up the street and then ditch the cup in a street bin. The support was what was important. Like a Good Samaritan.

Still, she couldn't fight the wave of bleakness that washed over her as she headed home. Even the gas lamps burning outside St. Mary's as evening fell rarely raised her spirits these days. She would often join the dwindling congregation and pray, more for Nigel to find his faith rather than the salvation of humanity. She'd leave that for the others. God's will was God's will. She had to trust it.

She heard the truck before she saw it – the loud, blaring *whoop-whoop* of the slow siren. The familiarity of the sound did nothing to stop the sudden tightness in her stomach and nervous leap of her heart. She glanced back and saw it round the corner from a side street and head toward her up the road. The few cars and buses behind it moved swiftly to the far side and came to a halt, whereas those in front picked up their pace. She didn't blame them. Despite her tiredness she increased her own pace. She knew an open cafe about hundred yards ahead, and wanted to get to it before the truck reached her.

The first rough hiss of the chemical spray blast made her flinch. Even though the truck was still some distance behind her the air almost immediately filled with the acrid scent. No way she wanted to be caught full on by that. The men in the truck wouldn't pause in their work to avoid hitting rare pedestrians. The spray was supposed to protect the public, which meant the population rather than the individual. Individuals no longer seemed to matter. She found the faceless masked soldiers and the spray somehow scarier than the plague itself. They were cold. Relentless.

Her nose itched with the stink and she took a shallow breath and held it as she broke into a jog, ignoring the aches in her tired legs, and instead focusing on the doorway ahead that bounced jerkily in her vision.

The *whoop-whoop* grew louder and she could hear the wheels trundling at their steady pace, catching up with her. She gritted her teeth. Couldn't the bastards see she was trying to get out of their path? Couldn't they just slow down for a second to let her get inside? She hadn't run for exercise – shit, she hadn't run at all – in a long time and she struggled to find a pace. She reached inside for her faith and pushed herself faster. Of course they wouldn't slow down. She didn't matter to them. So what if their poisons got in her lungs? This was why *He* was coming for them with his vengeance. Humanity had forgotten how to care for each other.

She slammed into the Mange Tout cafe door just as the truck burst a white cloud at her. She quickly closed it, leaning on it and sucking in deep breaths. The stench permeated through the gaps and hinges, but the door was solid and the building had thick, brick walls.

"You cut that fine," the young woman behind the counter said, her eyes focused on the street outside, her face tight and tense.

Abby didn't answer, but once she'd got her breath back she turned to look herself. The thick white fog blocked all sight of the road and the siren sounded like the call of a lost ghost ship as the truck moved on, the pavement disappearing into nothing, like a half-formed thought.

"Could I have a double espresso please?" she said.

Her throat was raw and she wondered whether from the running or the trails of insecticides that had caught up with her. Maybe both. She didn't want to think about it. Her body had enough problems without adding more. The government proclaimed over and over that the sprays were safe, but no one believed it. If that were the case, as one *Sunday Times* journalist had pointed out early on, why do the people driving the trucks, locked safely away inside, wear gas masks?

"They really think it's taking over here, don't they?" The coffee girl hadn't moved toward the machine. "Like in Brighton."

Abby said nothing. Of course the plague was taking over. How could they stop it? It was God's work.

Eventually, the girl made two coffees and the two women sat in silence sipping them until finally the fog outside turned to mist and then dissipated into nothing.

Half an hour later, Abby was nearly home. Behind the main thoroughfares, Islington sprawled into residential housing, the occasional block of flats, and long leafy streets of large Georgian terraced houses. The quiet here disturbed her less. It didn't seem quite so unnatural. At least she could persuade herself of that if she tried hard enough.

She shook her head as their home came into view. It had such beautiful lines but the blue netting tacked across the windows, draped across the front door and weighted down over the chimney had blurred and blunted them. It looked like a victim of renovation, or worse, repossession by the bank.

She climbed the steps, parted the netting, and quickly slipped through. In the blue mesh cocoon, she inspected the air around her. Finding it clear, she keyed open the door and darted through.

The window nets made the inside darker than it should have been, but not enough to turn on a light. She stripped down to her jeans and long-sleeved T-shirt and went to the kitchen where she followed George's instructions: found a dinner plate, opened the ring box, positioned it in the center, then placed the whole setup on a side table they never used.

She stared at the sac, nestled on the satin, and thought, I can't believe I'm doing this. I used to kill them, now I'm paying hundreds of pounds so I can bring them into my house.

The world had indeed turned upside down.

Knowing she couldn't put it off any longer, she headed for the spare bedroom. They'd called it "the baby's room" when they first moved in, but after that possibility died, it became "the office." It also served as the dialysis room, but who wanted to call it that? Certainly not Nigel. He couldn't even look at the machine.

She pulled the cover off the home hemodialysis unit. It stood four feet high and presented an array of screens, buttons, pumps, and meters she'd found daunting at first. Hanging the dialysate bags and plugging them in, testing the pressures and so on used to take forever, even with her nursing experience. But as time went on she became comfortable with the equipment. By now she could set it up and run it with her eyes closed.

She rolled up her left sleeve to expose the ropy fistula in her forearm. She sterilized the skin, plugged in the needles, then lay back in the recliner. Usually she read or watched TV, but the papers were playing up the plague for all it was worth, and the telly was playing it down, no doubt at the government's insistence. Don't want a full-scale panic now, do we? Didn't they ever go out on the streets? So today she simply stared at Nigel's desk against the far wall.

Nigel...gone nearly a week now, but due back tonight. She missed him – in more ways than one. A distance had grown between them. She wasn't the woman he'd married eight years ago – no denying the truth of that – but he'd changed too. When had it started? And why? She'd looked for the answers and kept coming back to her own private plague.

Things started to change when she'd discovered she had lupus.

She wondered how different it all might have been had places been reversed – with Nigel the sick one – but since lupus preferred women ten to one over men, that would have been unlikely.

It all started with swollen legs. Being a nurse, she'd self diagnosed the problem as too much salt. But when cutting back hadn't helped, she'd had one of the OBs she knew order some labs. Then the shock: Her kidneys were shot. A few more tests revealed lupus nephritis as the cause. She hadn't had any other symptoms – no rashes, no aches and pains, not a hint of anything wrong. The specialists started her on immunosuppressant therapy to save what was left of her kidneys.

Nigel hadn't handled it well. He kept wanting to blame someone or something – a polluting corporation or an environmental toxin. When Abby had informed him it was God's doing, he'd almost exploded.

But it was. She'd known that almost immediately. Despite a strict Catholic upbringing, she'd allowed herself to become a doubter and had fallen away from the Church. It started in nursing school – exposure to all that death and disease had sparked questions as to any sort of Divine Plan. The doubts smoldered until she'd simply discarded her faith like an old skin.

But God had been watching, as He always was, and He sent her an autoimmune wake-up call.

So the lupus was her own doing and she was dealing with it as best she could. She'd returned to the Church, went to mass every day, and tried to help Nigel to see the light. The first two were easy. Bringing Nigel to the Church – or to any kind of faith, for that matter – seemed nigh impossible. But "nigh" was the important word there. For no soul was beyond redemption. She prayed for Nigel every day.

But now maybe she should pray for the world as well.

She prayed for Nigel's safe return. He'd been sent to Africa. Well, *sent* really hadn't been the case, had it. Truth was, he'd begged Mal to put him on the story. Abby hadn't wanted him to go. Yes-yes, she knew he was an investigative journalist and all that, and he couldn't very well turn his back on the story of the millennium, but he was journeying into the belly of the beast for "the truth" when it was right in front of him.

St. Mark had it so right: *Do you have eyes but fail to see, and ears but fail to hear?*

Just as God had sent her a personal wake-up call, He was now sending one to all humanity: *Mene, Mene, Tekel u-Pharsin* had been inscribed on the wall of the world in the form of a plague. The message was clear to Abby: Change your ways and come together to fight this, or all shall suffer my Holy Wrath.

But the world was either blind to the writing on the wall or ignoring its warning. Instead of finding fellowship and community against a common enemy, humanity was further fragmenting as people pointed fingers and locked themselves away for protection.

She felt drowsy. She never slept well when she was alone in the house. She didn't want to nap but let her eyes close… just to rest them a little.

IS PARIS BURNING?

PORT SAINT-OUEN – Raging Muslim rioters are rampaging on the streets of the French capital setting fire to cars in protest as the government tries to stop boatloads of terrified Algerians crossing the Mediterranean in anything that will float. Efforts to quell this plague-driven flood of people to France's shores have left the Mediterranean coast awash in North Africans who can't go forward or back. (The Daily Express)

NIGEL

With the aid of several glasses of champagne, Nigel had managed to sleep at least half the way to London, which wasn't bad given how wired he'd been when he got on the plane. But now that he'd come down the gantry and through the first wave of sprays, he was feeling tired, edgy and mildly dehydrated. Within half an hour a headache would be kicking in, the kind that sat somewhere between stress and a hangover, and by the time he got home his mood would be foul. Not the way he wanted to greet Abby.

At least flying business class he'd got to the immigration lines ahead of the rest. He forced a smile as a dour-faced woman sprayed him once again before letting him wait for the passport officer to examine his documents. Always a tricky business knowing just how friendly to act; drawing any attention to yourself either way could get you hauled off for a full body search and several hours of questioning. Heathrow was brimming with immigration men and police, all wired and hard on the lookout for potential threats.

Nigel's reputation with the paper would count for shit if he gave the wrong man the wrong look at the wrong time. As far as the authorities were concerned, terrorists came from every potential walk of life. Despite what some people believed, you could never tell a man's god from his appearance. These days, everyone was a potential zealot.

He took a small moment's pleasure from seeing the man who had sat next to him now several places back in a parallel queue and looking tired and disheveled. No surprise there. When Nigel had stopped drinking and finally relaxed enough to fall asleep, the other man must have continued throughout the flight. He'd been pretty much passed out before awakened by the stewardess asking them to fasten their seatbelts. If Nigel was feeling the beginnings of a mild headache, then this bloke must be facing a belter of a hangover. It almost made Nigel feel sorry for him. Almost, but not quite. His reserves of pity had fallen low over the past few months, and he wasn't going to waste any on an over-privileged idiot soaked in champagne and bigotry.

He made it through passport control relatively easily and, after a final seal and spray in a Plexiglas cubicle, he wandered down to the baggage hall. Restrictions had been placed on flights from several international destinations, and so Heathrow terminal 5, the hub of British Airways, was relatively quiet. Outbound flights were fewer and fewer. Almost everywhere was worse than here.

He waited at the carousel until he saw his tan bag appear and then fought his way through the small crowd to reach it. So far, not so bad. He was going to make it through the airport in less than two hours, something of a miracle these days.

He passed through the nothing-to-declare aisle and headed into the main terminal, his eyes scanning for a coffee booth. He had a good hour's cab ride into Central London and he wasn't going to make it without a double cappuccino and plenty of sugar. Abby drank espressos. She didn't mess around where caffeine was concerned, and back in the early days before she got sick it became a joke between them. Everywhere they ordered, they got served each other's drinks. Gender stereotyping in hot beverages. Imagine.

He ordered his drink and as he waited he realized just how long ago those days seemed now. Shit, they *were* a long time ago. They'd had a lot more sickness than health in their relationship.

He took the cup from the spotty, teenage waiter and went to the counter to add his three sugars before heading toward the black cab rank. So intent on his destination, he didn't see the thin, suited man until he barged past Nigel and knocked his arm. The bump sent the hot liquid all over his shirt, scalding his skin beneath.

"Jesus Christ," he said, turning viciously on the man. "Can't you just watch where you're going?"

He wasn't in the mood for this. He looked down at the brown stain across the middle of his white shirt. He'd be changing in the cab then.

"Sorry, sorry. I'm truly sorry."

Nigel looked. The man might be apologizing but his eyes darted this way and that. Along the line of wispy, thinning hair on his forehead, drops of sweat shone in the unnatural light.

"Are you okay?"

Something about the man was making the hairs on the back of his neck prickle. Something off. Nigel had weathered enough shitty situations to know that when something felt badly wrong, it nearly always was.

"They're moving," he said with barely repressed glee.

"What?"

The man licked his lips as they parted in a sickly smile. "I can feel them! They're *moving!*"

He shuffled forward, somewhere between a jog and a walk, heading toward the exit. Wet shirt and coffee forgotten, Nigel looked around for a security guard. Had anyone else noticed how odd this man was behaving, or were all the guards and cameras focused on people *before* they got out into the main terminal building?

He dumped his coffee in a bin and walked faster to catch the man up.

"I said, are you okay?"

He grabbed his arm – little more than skin-coated bone. The man turned and for the first time Nigel realized that maybe the thinning hair had nothing to do with age and everything to do with treatment. Now that they were close, he could almost smell the sickness under the rancid stale sweat. Cancer? Was that the cause of the tension coming off this man in waves?

"I'm sorry," the man repeated, licking his lips. "I'm really sorry."

He began to roll up one sleeve, and in that moment Nigel saw the flash of the golden crucifix at his neck.

"No," Nigel said, as the pieces started to slot into place.

Paris. This was Paris all over again. The apology wasn't for him. It was meant for everyone.

The man pulled away, his rolled sleeve now exposing the sutures beneath. Nigel lunged forward but the man ran to the doorway, stopping just at the place where the electronic doors opened. Summer heat rushed to greet them.

"Don't you fucking dare!"

The man launched his small bag at Nigel and his feet tangled in the strap, bringing him down hard on his knees. He wasn't going to make it.

A few people had turned to see what the fuss was, but they were like sheep, dazed and tired from traveling and eager to get on their way. The thin man fixed his gaze on Nigel as he tore at the sutures holding the flaps of his skin together.

Nigel knew what was coming.

The world slowed. Somewhere, several feet away, two security guards turned. They frowned and then their eyes widened. The older of the two reached for the holster at his side but his fingers fumbled on the button-down flap. Out of practice. The other simply froze and stared before reaching for his walkie-talkie.

"Shoot him!" Nigel said. "Stop him!"

But he knew whatever they were going to do, they'd be too late.

Behind them, through the door from the baggage reclaim, came the irritating smug fool from the plane, huffing and puffing as he pushed his overladen trolley.

You're going to find out first hand, Nigel thought as he watched him. Goodbye Paris, hello London. And look, it's a white guy. Take that, you twat.

"I'm so sorry," the thin man sobbed as he flinched and ripped back the now loose skin of his inner arm. "But you'll thank me later when He comes to you."

Nigel met his eyes. Fear. Madness. A sudden moment of doubt maybe. It was all there. And still he tore. No going back now.

The man's fingers were bloody from ripping out the sutures, but the exposed flesh beneath appeared covered with small dark brown ovals crammed so tightly together that they didn't tumble out when exposed to the air. Some were still stuck to the flap of skin the man held open.

A woman standing a few feet away screamed. Nigel didn't blame her. Anyone close enough to see knew what they were looking at. The posters littered Britain. One of the stages of development – the most likely to be smuggled stage.

Pupae. They'd been stitched under the thin man's skin and now here they were, ready to hatch. Nigel's eyes narrowed and his heart raced as he saw a tiny speck disengage from the pack, and then a second and a third. No, not *ready* to hatch – hatching.

His fellow passenger had nearly reached the doors with his trolley, one of the few people around who wasn't still frozen in that moment of shock. His sense of self-preservation was pretty good, he'd give him that. But Nigel should have known that from the fact he'd made it onto the plane out of Cairo. The trolley trundled onward, the man now almost running, his mouth hanging open as he gasped in breath, physical exertion obviously not in his normal routine.

Nigel watched it happen almost in slow motion. One of the flies, so recently hatched, darted this way and that through the air. The passenger didn't see it, his eyes focused on the door and getting out. His mouth hung open. The fly buzzed. The two collided.

There was an old lady who swallowed a fly, I don't know why she swallowed a fly, perhaps she'll die.

The trolley had stopped. The passenger was spitting and swiping at his face, strange panicked mewling sounds coming from him as he did. A gunshot finally rang out and Nigel spun round to see the thin man crumple to the floor, the hatching pupae still drifting away from their hiding place inside him.

The airport descended into screaming chaos, people rushing toward Nigel to get to the closing doors. He hauled himself to his feet. The doors weren't just closing, someone somewhere safe at the other end of the security cameras was shutting down the airport.

Not with me in it, he thought. Not with what I have in my pocket.

He lunged forward, the passenger and the carrier momentarily forgotten and threw himself into the narrowing gap.

The doors thudded behind him and he raced to the taxi rank. He didn't look back. He didn't need to.

BBC:

This from Mumbai – reports of clouds of flies darkening the skies and mass burnings outside the city as bodies are bulldozed into piles and set ablaze to prevent them from becoming breeding grounds for more flies. We are trying to bring you video but communications from the subcontinent are sporadic at best.

AT "THE LIGHT"

"One man's responsible for all this? Is that what you're saying?" Malcolm Brown shook his head. "I can't believe it."

They sat in Mal's darkened office with the door closed. Nigel had taken charge of Mal's computer. Edmund Toulson, caricature of a publisher with his big belly, braces, and suit pants, slouched to his right. Mal, his black skin gleaming in the glow from the monitor, hunched forward on his left.

"I'm not saying that at all," Nigel said. "All I'm saying is that Rajiv Singh designed and led the TSEE Project."

Toulson harrumphed. "We're dealing with some sort of mad scientist then? We can run with that, can't we, Mal?"

Mal nodded. "We can get a marathon out of that—"

"Wait-wait-wait!" Nigel tried to keep his voice even. Had they been listening at all?"

As soon as he'd arrived in the London *Light*'s office, he copied his thumb drive onto his desk computer. He could have sent it by email but the contents were too sensitive to trust to the Internet. Not these days. He'd forwarded the data to Mal's via the *Light*'s LAN so they could confer with Toulson in private.

"Let me go over this again. Doctor Singh was heading a project that exposed male tsetse flies to gamma rays—"

Toulson waved his hands toward the monitor. "Now why in God's name would anyone do that?"

The after-effects of too much champagne and too little sleep had frayed Nigel's nerves. He wanted to scream *Weren't you listening the first time through?* But he maintained outer calm.

"To sterilize them. The female tsetse fly mates and stores the sperm for future use. If that sperm is sterile, she can't fertilize any of her eggs. As a result, the tsetse fly population drops. Fewer tsetse flies mean fewer deaths from trypanosomiasis."

When Toulson looked puzzled, Mal added, "Sleeping sickness."

Toulson's features morphed to an I-knew-that expression. "Right. Of course. But the plague isn't sleeping sickness and tsetse flies aren't the problem – at least that's what I'm told."

"Correct," Nigel said. "The vector is a new species of biting fly."

Mal leaned forward. "Nigel believes Doctor Singh's project created a mutation in another species that became the vector fly."

"On purpose?"

"No," Nigel said. "Everything I've learned about the man says we've got no mad scientist scenario here."

Toulson's crushed look was almost comical. "You're sure? Absolutely *sure*? Remember when those barmy Dutch blokes mutated the bird flu to make it even more contagious? You sure we don't have something like that going on here?"

Oh, you'd love that, wouldn't you, Nigel thought. You'd sell a *lot* of papers with that.

Edmund Toulson had inherited the London *Light* from his father, along with his father's knack for snappy headlines. Sadly he lacked his father's intelligence and learning. The result was a popular tabloid with more substance than most, but only because of Malcolm's editorial acumen.

As for making the H_5N_1 avian flu airborne – Nigel saw that as the height of scientific arrogance:

Why would you do such a bloody stupid thing?
Because we can!

"Quite sure. The whole thrust of TSEE Project was humanitarian – to eradicate a disease. But when you're out netting flies, looking for male tsetses, is it a big stretch to imagine other species finding their way into the mix and being irradiated as well? So a couple of other flies get sterilized along with the tsetses. No big deal, right? That only means fewer flies to annoy you."

Mal was nodding. "But what if they *don't* get sterilized?

Mal got it. He always got it. That was why Nigel loved him.

"Right. What if these gamma rays instead trigger a mutation that leads to a new species that spreads a plague among humanity?"

Toulson rubbed his chin. "The best of intentions with unintended consequences of the worst possible sort. We can go with that. This Singh bloke did it. We'll–"

"Wait," Nigel said. "We can't demonize the man. He's not evil."

"Says who?" Toulson said. "We need somebody to point to, and he's perfect. I mean really, what right did he have to go and mess with the stuff of Creation?"

Nigel made a face. He'd expect something like that from Abby. "Stuff of Creation?"

"Yes! DNA!"

"He wasn't messing with DNA! He was there to fry fly balls, that's all. I have no direct proof that he caused a mutation."

Toulson rolled his eyes. "Then why are we having this conversation?"

"Because I'm close. I've got a ton of circumstantial evidence."

Mal grabbed a pen and grabbed a lined notepad. "Like?"

"The TSEE Project was discontinued three years ago. It worked beautifully in Zanzibar, which is virtually tsetse free now, but that's an island. Sub-Saharan Africa is a whole other story. More people die of *nagana* there" – he glanced at Toulson – "sleeping sickness, than HIV. Singh had temporary success, but then funding ran out and he returned to London."

"Where was he doing this sterilizing?" Mal said, pen poised.

"Salonga National Park."

"Where's that?" Toulson said.

"The Congo." Mal's eyes widened. "Jesus, Nigel, the first reported cases of the plague were in the Congo basin."

"Right. Two and a half years ago…six months after Singh shut down."

Toulson pounded the desktop. "Then we've *got* him! He fooled with Mother Nature and six months later the plague began. What more do you need?"

Nigel glanced at Mal. "*Post hoc ergo propter hoc.*" He waited for Toulson's inevitable response and wasn't disappointed.

"What's that supposed to mean?"

Mal said, "It's Latin. Means: *After this, therefore because of this.* It's a famous logical fallacy in that it assumes if B follows A, then A caused B."

Toulson shrugged. "Thunder follows lightning."

"And pain follows a punch in the face," Nigel said, wishing he could do just that. "And sometimes a rainstorm follows dancing around a fire. But that doesn't mean the dance caused the rain." He pushed on before Toulson could add another inane comment. "What I'm saying is, we can't paint a man as a death-bringer who makes Hitler and Stalin look like pikers until we have a definite link."

"And where do we get that link? If this bastard's the culprit, I want the *Light* to break it."

"When I was in Africa I overnighted some of the dead flies to an entomologist at the museum. I've asked him to see if he can determine whether or not the species is a recent mutation. If it is, we'll have opportunity, and proximity as to both time and space. I'll feel justified then in pointing the finger of suspicion – and it can be suspicion only – at Doctor Rajiv Singh."

Mal and Toulson spoke almost in unison: "When will we know?"

After a quick laugh, Nigel said, "Tomorrow, I hope."

"Can we trust him?" Toulson said.

"What do you mean?"

"I mean, he won't put out a press release or anything, will he? He'll come to us first, right?"

"Well, I'm – or rather, *you're* paying his fee. And I promised him full credit for his opinion."

Toulson slapped the desktop with both hands. "Brilliant! Key it up and have it ready to go as soon as we hear from him." He rose and patted Nigel on the shoulder. "Good work, son."

Nigel watched him leave, almost tripping over the janitor who was mopping the floor outside Mal's office.

"A 'good work' from Toulson. Sort of like 'good voice' from Lou Reed."

Mal laughed. "Get writing and have it ready."

"It's written. Let's get a drink. I need a proper gin."

AT THE WHITE HART

"Earth to Nigel."

Nigel looked up in time to see Mal placing a gin and lime before him.

"Got you a double," Mal added as he seated himself. "You look like you could use it."

"Very much so. Been a little bit too much going on for one day." He lifted his glass to clink it against Mal's pint but stopped. "Stout?"

Mal shrugged. "They've run out of bitter."

Nigel had never known the White Hart to run out of anything.

"Well, in spite of that, cheers."

After a gulp, Mal said, "Where was your head just now? Africa? Or Heathrow?"

"Heathrow's over and done with. Not like it was anything we didn't expect, I was just unlucky to be there."

"And what was that crazy thinking? The flies are already here in droves."

Nigel pictured his feverish face. "Maybe he didn't know that. Maybe he was committing suicide by copper. Whatever, it's Africa that's stuck in my head."

Here in the White Hart, just around the corner from the *Light's* offices, life seemed perfectly normal. Well, almost. The mosquito netting over the windows and doors was new, but that hadn't seemed to thin the usual crowd of staffers from the paper. Maybe because the flies weren't active in the dark.

"How was it? As bad as we've heard?"

Nigel shook his head. "No matter what you've heard, no matter how many hours of film you've seen, nothing can prepare you for the reality of it."

"Want to talk about it?"

No, he did not. But maybe he should. Maybe he should spew some of this before he went home to Abby. He couldn't tell her what he'd seen. At least not uncensored. Too horrible. And she would filter whatever he did tell her through her *Weltanshauung* of Divine Providence and then they'd fight again.

So he gave Mal the whole story.

———————

The Democratic Republic of the Congo had been silent for weeks, just like most of the rest of sub-Saharan Africa. Other governments from Europe and the US and Russia had sent in teams and then withdrawn them without releasing information. Toulson had sent Nigel to learn what they were hiding.

He hired a private plane with an Egyptian pilot who was either crazy or desperate for cash or both, and they flew into Ndolo Airport in Kinshasa, formerly Leopoldville, on the border of the Congo and what was formerly Zaire. Everything in central Africa seemed formerly something else.

And now, it had earned another formerly: populated.

The airport was unresponsive but its beacon was still transmitting, enabling the pilot to find it with no difficulty. He landed without clearance because none was forthcoming from the empty control tower.

The pilot didn't want to leave the plane, but Nigel dragged him into town. He wasn't risking returning to the airport and finding him gone. Wearing hooded white contamination suits, they commandeered a car from a rental lot. They could have walked – the airport was near the heart of the city – but the air was hot as Hades and Nigel wanted to be enclosed. So they drove into the city in air-conditioned comfort.

Kinsasha, the capital of the DRC, the second largest city in Africa after Cairo, home to ten million souls, had flies everywhere – peppering the walls of all the buildings, hazing the air – but no people. The flies seemed oblivious to the car and its passengers. Perhaps because the contamination suits locked in their scent.

Where was everyone? Cattle and chickens and dogs wandered the streets, but no people. The fly bites had no effect on animals, other than a mild irritation. If a God was at work, then he'd decided that man needed to go, not the rest of the world's fauna. Nigel couldn't entirely blame him for that, although Mother Nature was a more likely culprit. Mother Nature and mankind working hand in hand to bring about their own destruction. If it wasn't so terrifying, it would be comical.

At one point they spotted a human – someone immune to the plague? – who ran and hid at sight of them. Only rarely did they see any dead, signaled by an extra-thick cloud of flies.

The pilot pointed out a huge cloud beyond a stand of trees.

"What do you suppose that is?" he said, voice muffled by the air filters in his hood.

Against his better judgment, Nigel said, "Let's find out," and headed for the cloud.

He found a two-story building literally coated with flies, with those unable to land buzzing around it. Gut knotted, he wound his way past abandoned cars, wondering what he'd found. Halfway to the building he came upon a white stone sign. The flies left enough room to read:

REPUBLIQUE DEMOCRATIQUE DU CONGO
MINISTERE DE LA SANTE
HOSPITAL PEDIATRIQUE DE
KALEMBE - LEMBE

Aw, no. A children's hospital.

He closed his eyes, took a few deep breaths, then said, "I'm going in."

"Yaha!" the pilot cried.

"What?" Nigel knew only enough Arabic to ask for a beer or a bathroom.

The pilot stared at him. "Are you daft?"

"Most likely."

But this was why he'd come. He jumped out of the car, taking the keys with him.

"Hey!" the pilot yelled. "I'll cook in here!"

"I won't be long."

"What if something happens to you?"

"I won't go far."

He'd traveled only a dozen feet when the smell of death smashed him, slipping through his air filter and tickling his gag reflex. He swallowed back a surge of bile and pressed on.

Then the rotting bodies began to appear, more and more until he found them massed at the doors. All in advanced states of decay.

What had happened here?

The plague, for all its virulence, was reported to be gentle. People didn't drop in the street. They grew progressively weaker until they took to their beds, never to rise again. Was that what happened here?

Beneath the coating of flies he made out many small bodies among the larger ones. Ailing children, brought to the hospital by their equally ailing parents, where they all died, waiting for admission to a hospital big enough for no more than a hundred beds.

Through breaks in the clouds of flies he saw the feasting maggots, which would soon mature and join the cloud. And as digestible flesh disappeared, the cloud would move, looking for greener pastures, as it were.

He turned and fled to the car, and then to the airport, and then back to Cairo.

———————

"Jesus," Mal murmured, his pint warming in his hand.

Nigel tossed back his gin. "Yeah. It's the life cycle of those damn flies that's against us. One bite is all it takes and you've caught the plague. Three days later, you're dead. But if no one buries you, you become a fly factory. Each of the little bastards lays scores of eggs on the corpse. Those hatch into maggots, feed on the carrion, turn into flies, mate, lay more eggs, and on and on."

"A geometric progression."

"But not a simple doubling progression. Each generation progresses by a factor of a hundred. They were multiplying like crazy in the jungles and no one knew. Then they swarmed into the unsuspecting cities in a cloud and no one was prepared, no one had a chance. So more die – so many that the urban services break down and bodies are left where they drop, which only further feeds the swarm."

"I can't believe no one's got a way of stopping them. Can't we import a bunch of toads or insectivorous birds?"

"From where? Who's going to give them up? The only real threats to flies are spiders and parasites, and these African flies don't have any local parasites."

"There's got to be *something*."

Nigel shook his head. "Not yet."

Everyone thought the desert would stop them because they seemed to like a moist environment. But they followed the Nile and from there they spread everywhere, especially after the Mungus started capturing them and shipping them across the oceans.

Mal's expression was bleak. "Then we're fucked?"

"We thought we'd be safe because we're an island–"

"Are we really?" Mal said with a tight smile. "I never realized." The smile vanished. "Things exploded while you were away. When the first few Londoners came down with it, a mob charged into the hospital and dragged them out on the street where they doused them with gas and set them alight."

Speechless, Nigel could only stare at him. When he regained his voice...

"That's – that's appalling! It's not contagious! Everyone knows that."

"Apparently not. Or if they do, they don't believe it. Government propaganda, government conspiracy, government cover-up – take your choice. It spreads like AIDS, it spreads like flu, it's being blown into the air and the flies are just a diversion, misdirection to keep us from learning what's *really* going on."

He supposed that was because modern medical science, with all its miracles, had yet to get a handle on the plague. Bites from the flies didn't transmit a disease – a virus would have been easy to fight. Instead, fly saliva, even in the minutest amount, triggered an autoimmune reaction that targeted the victim's red blood cells. The result was a fulminate hemolytic anemia that stressed nearly every organ in the body and overwhelmed the marrow's ability to replace the dissolving red cells. Eventually death comes from hypoxia and systemic collapse – without red blood cells to carry oxygen to the organs, they fail. Transfusions give only temporary relief because the immune system attacks the new red blood cells upon arrival.

Mal said, "Blood banks have all run dry and they're staying dry. I mean, where do you find blood donors when everyone knows they won't have enough of their own if they're bitten?"

Fighting a sudden wave of exhaustion – physical and spiritual – Nigel shook his head. "Why am I not surprised?"

"Wait. It gets worse. The Mungus are wandering about, and they take the opposite view: The plague is God's retribution. Don't fight it – accept it. And so we've got believers exposing themselves to the flies and going off to die and supply breeding grounds for more flies. Those who remain untouched by the plague were welcomed into the Mungu cult. Needless to say – but I'll say it anyway – its numbers are minuscule."

"Damn them."

Mungu…Swahili for *divine*. An exclusive membership – limited to survivors of the plague. The theory was they were gifted with a natural immunity. Early members were all African. When they lived on while all around them died, the only rationale – at least as they saw it – was that God had chosen them to spread the word that the plague was His doing: divine retribution. Now plague survivors of all races called themselves Mungu.

Mal said, "I'd love to get video from Brighton."

"I could go down."

"They've shut down all of Sussex. But why? The plague's everywhere. They've been lying about how far it's spread." Mal stared at him for a long moment, then, "Anyway, I think you've had enough plague for a while."

"*What?*" He couldn't believe he'd heard right.

"I'm serious. You should see yourself. You look shredded. You've visited hell. You need a break."

"Mal, this is the story of the century – the bloody millennium! What could be more important?"

"A change of pace. For the sake of your sanity. There's a missing child–"

"A child? *One* child? People are dying by the millions, Mal. I don't mean to sound callous, but–"

"It's my wife's cousin's little boy – he's gone missing and the police aren't doing shit."

"I'm sorry for them, Mal, really I am, but–"

"There's a story there, Nigel. I can smell it."

Mal's nose for stories was well known, almost infamous, but still…

"Maybe after I see if I can get into Sussex." As he finished the last of his gin he glanced at the TV over the bar. Flames filled the screen. "Here, what's that?"

Mal needed only a quick glance. "Berlin's burning."

"What?"

"The crazies do it. At night they set the residential districts alight, driving people out into the streets. When daylight comes they've got no homes to go to, and so the flies get them."

Cairo had been burning. Same thing?

"Did everyone go mad while I was away?"

"Appears that way."

Nigel rose from his seat. Really could have used another gin, but… "Hate to drink and run, but I've gotta get home to Abby. It's been a week."

"After Sussex then? You promise?"

"Sure."

Did that sound like a promise? He hoped not.

NIGEL

Strange how his mood could shift between turning the key in the lock and closing the door behind him. He'd been looking forward to seeing Abby. They'd been fine on the phone while he was away, almost like the old days, but as soon as he felt the latch turn, so did his stomach. His shoulders tensed as the warm, familiar smell of home hit him, and by the time he'd put his suitcase down in the hall, he couldn't fight the unease. The awkwardness.

No…tonight would be different. Tonight they'd be the old Nigel and Abby.

"I'm home," he called out, resisting the urge simply to go quietly into the kitchen and make himself a drink and have a few more minutes alone.

All shit and he knew it. He loved her. He'd always loved her. But that didn't mean he found it easy facing her. Not these days, anyway. Bad enough when she'd got sick, but worse now. Sickness outside, and sickness inside. Sometimes he felt so surrounded by it that death seemed to be crawling on his skin trying to find a way in. It all made him feel like a selfish bastard – shit, he *was* a selfish bastard – and then that made him resentful for feeling that way.

Marriage, he thought, as he heard the light tread of her steps coming down the stairs, was never the bed of roses the movies made it out to be. These days, no matter how flirtatious they got when they were apart, it was barely a bed at all.

"Hey," Abby said as she landed in the hall. Although only in jeans and a T-shirt – long sleeved, thank you – she was wearing pink lipstick and her hair looked freshly washed and dried, falling loose around her shoulders. "Welcome home, traveler."

She wrapped her arms around his neck and smiled. Warm perfume wafted over him, mixed with the soft scent of her he knew so well. It very nearly disguised the underlying hint of something other. The *unwell*, the thing he found so hard to fight.

"Hey."

He squeezed her back, wishing he could hug his shame away, but instead he had to fight the urge to pull back. He wondered if she could feel it. The strain in his arms.

He pressed his face into her neck and planted a dry kiss there. Where her T-shirt had slipped slightly on her shoulder he could see the black bra strap beneath. He recognized it – part of a set she'd bought from Agent Provocateur the last year. The lipstick. The underwear. Oh Abby. So hopeful. And yet the jeans and T-shirt. Scared to push too hard.

Yes, he really was a bastard. Was his wife this nervous with him now?

If only they could go back in time to how it used to be. They'd been so *good* together.

"I'm shattered," he said. That's it, Nigel – set up the excuses early. Not that it'll hurt her any less when you roll over and face the other way. "The flight was hell, and then that crap at Heathrow, never mind having to go and debrief at the office."

"But you're home now." She stepped back, still smiling. "I've even cooked you dinner. Lasagna. From scratch. Who says the traditional wife is dead? Come on, I've got a bottle of red open. You look like you need it."

He followed her into the kitchen, watching her slim frame move with the same sensual rhythm that had caught his eye the first time he'd seen her. He was the problem, not her. She was the one who was sick but he was the one who couldn't cope. In the main, Abby coped just fine. She even looked the same, give or take a lost pound or two. But the goddamn lupus was always *there*. And try as he might he couldn't forgive it for stalking her.

He avoided looking as they passed the small study to the left of the kitchen that had become the dialysis room, but that didn't stop him feeling the claustrophobic pressure of knowing what was in there.

Why couldn't she at least shut the bloody door on it? Hide it like those long sleeves hid that wormy fistula on her forearm? Make it easier for him to pretend everything was fine.

"Thanks," he said, taking the large glass of Merlot she handed him.

Another drink would help. Always did. He felt a sudden pang of loss in his heart. He missed their getting drunk together. After everything he'd seen while away, he could use a little getting drunk and laughing like they used to. He missed their carefree days. He missed his wife, even though she was standing right in front of him.

"You going to join me?"

He cursed himself before the question was fully out. What was he doing? Baiting her illness?

"I'll have one with dinner. You know how it is." Her eyes darkened slightly but she busied herself at the oven. "I was so worried when I saw about the airport on the news. Thank God you texted me. I thought you were stuck in there."

"I was lucky."

He sipped more of the wine. He was drinking too quickly given that he already had a buzz on from the pub, but this wasn't a conversation he wanted to have with Abby. How could he rage at her about the God Squad idiots trying to spread this shit? How could he talk to her about any of it without getting into some kind of argument? They couldn't talk about her illness and they sure as shit couldn't talk about his work and the plague. He wished the BBC would throw up some new drama. Maybe then their conversation could at least pretend not have run dry.

"I got the thing you wanted," she said as she took two plates down from the shelf.

"Thing?"

"You know." She busied herself with cutlery and oven gloves and didn't look him in the eye. "The egg sac." She said the last words as if she were spilling her illness onto him. "It's on the table in the sitting room." Finally, she glanced up at him. "He tried to charge me an extra hundred but I said no."

"But you got what we ordered?"

His stomach unfurled slightly. His house felt safer already, even if they hadn't hatched yet.

"I got what you ordered, yes."

And there it was. The sting. Maybe tonight their argument wouldn't be his fault. He hadn't even mentioned her God. Not once.

"They could save our lives, Abs. They're worth the money." He sounded reasonable and he was glad of it. "I know you don't like spiders, but Jesus, if you'd seen what I've seen this week, you'd want them in bed with you."

"It would be nice to have something in bed with me, that's for sure." She slapped a heavy spoonful of pasta onto one plate. "And if you want to swear then there are other words to choose."

Oh, please let's not do this.

"Just an expression, Abby."

"For someone who doesn't believe in Him, you take His name in vain enough."

They'd been through this...how many times?

"I was raised just as Catholic as you, and that's all I heard. You must've too, because I've heard your dad after he's had a couple."

"At least he believes."

"And that makes it okay?"

She faltered a second – just a second – as she dealt another dose of pasta onto a second plate. "That makes it less not okay. But let's talk about something else."

"Please, let's."

———

After a hurried gobbling of wine and pasta – really, she was a good cook – between stilted attempts at conversation, dinner ended and he helped her clean up. As they wandered through the sitting room, she paused at the side table.

"Oh, look. Your babies have arrived."

Nigel joined her and peered over her shoulder at the plate. When he'd first looked, just a moment before dinner, it had resembled a small muddy pearl sitting in a ring box. Now the pearl had developed what appeared to be a faint haze. He leaned closer and saw a milling cloud of tiny beige spiders with black spots on their butts.

"Spiderlings."

He'd always had a love-hate relationship with spiders. He loved how they fed on pesky insects, especially flies; the way they'd leap upon trapped prey and wrap them in webbing fascinated him. But the way they moved, vertically and horizontally, seeming to glide on their eight speedy legs, gave him major creeps.

Now, however, with what was going on in the world outside, he adored them.

Abby said, "Now what?"

He straightened. "Time to deploy the troops."

"Now?"

"I want to separate them before they start munching on their siblings."

She shuddered. "I thought just the mother did that."

"Sometimes. But either way, these little buggers have got to eat. And considering what they cost, I don't want them tucking into each other."

He pulled the stepladder from the closet, then a couple of teaspoons from the drawer.

"I'll take the upper corners," he said, handing her a spoon. "You take the lower. We'll have this done in a trice."

"'Trice'?" She smiled, and for an instant he sensed the old Abby peek through. "Did you just say 'trice'?"

"I believe I did. Where did that come from?"

Truly he had no idea. They laughed together for a moment at the absurdity of the word and it felt good.

He scooped up a few spiderlings in his spoon and climbed into one of the upper corners of the kitchen. He felt unsteady up here. Perhaps this wasn't the best time, after gin and wine and all, but he couldn't let them eat each other.

He pressed the tip of the spoon against the wall there and let the babies crawl off the silver onto the plaster. Even if they wandered off, he assumed at least one of them would return, since they seemed to prefer setting up their webs in corners. Too bad those webs wouldn't be big enough to threaten flies for a while, but he had to start somewhere.

When he returned to the floor he found Abby standing by the plate, spoon in hand, right where he'd left her.

"Come on, have at it," he said. "Or our trice will become a... what?"

She was shaking her head. "I don't think I can do this."

He understood. "Look, I don't like spiders either, but they're an extra line of defense."

"Against what?"

"Against the flies."

"I think you mean against God."

Uh-oh. Here we go. Their shared laugh of moments ago was now dust.

"It's not God who'll bite you."

Flippant, he knew, but what the hell did she expect him to say?

"The flies are God's doing."

"Really? There I was thinking it was a monumental human fuckup that had brought this on us. Come on, Abby. I've been working on this since it started. This is people. Not God."

She stepped closer, her eyes pleading. "Don't you see the symmetry? Humans came out of Africa. So did the flies. God's hand."

"Passover was God's hand too, I believe. Let's consider the spiders akin to splashing a little lamb's blood over the door. And as for Adam and Eve, I thought they came from the Garden of Eden. Was that in Africa?"

He was getting angry, and he couldn't help it. Perhaps he should be trying to appease her, but after everything he'd seen in the last week, the one thing he couldn't take was her high and mighty God-is-great mentality. Mentality. Mental. She certainly sounded that way these days.

"Give me a little credit, will you." She looked a bit angry herself now. "I'm not one of those fundamentalist nuts. I don't take the Bible literally. I know damn well the Earth wasn't created in six days four thousand years ago."

"More like six thousand," he said.

"What?"

"Bishop Ussher's date was 4004 BC"

"You *know* that?"

"Idiots amuse me."

Why don't I just shut up?

Her face darkened. "Well, I'm not an idiot. I believe in evolution. But I also believe it was guided."

"You can't have it both ways. You think some omnipresent God sent the flies but evolution is fine? What about God is great, God is good? If your God is so good then why the hell is he trying to wipe us out? He doesn't need to lift a finger to do that. Just give us time. Look at history! We're good enough at doing that for ourselves."

He refilled his wineglass. Alcohol wasn't going to help anything, but if he was going to have this argument at the end of a day like today, then he was going to have it with wine.

"Did it ever occur to you that God is fed up with us? To quote you: Look at history. Look what we've done to each other. He's cleaning up his house. And the fact that He's doing it with flies shows how disgusted He is with us!"

"Ever since you got sick you've been looking for meaning in everything. It's shit that you're ill. I hate that you're ill." There – the closest he'd ever got to an admission of that in the whole time the awful dialysis machine had hulked in the next room. "But it all comes down to cells and structures and bad fucking luck. We live in chaos, Abby. The universe is chaos, and man is a result of that and this so-called plague is the result of man's stupidity."

"You always do this," she said, shaking her head in that

condescending way that drove him up the wall. "You want to bring everything down to the dirt. You never look up. Heaven is in charge, Nigel. It keeps its hand hidden, it moves behind the scenes, but it's always moving. Except for now. Now it's out in the open. This is like the Great Flood – and there *was* a great flood in olden times, Nigel. Every religion has an ancient Great Flood. It was a cleansing, and so is this. Can't you see that?"

"Maybe it *is* a cleansing. But if so, then nature's doing it, not some invisible friend." He stared at his wife. A stranger before him. "If you're such a fan of God's will, then why do you plug yourself into that machine every day? Why doesn't he save you? You're spreading enough p-r for him, you'd think it'd be the least he could do?"

Behind the red of his rage, he wondered when he'd become so cruel.

"God tests us," she said levelly. "Like he did Job. And God helps those who help themselves. I'm being tested and I'm responding the best I can." Sudden tears rimmed her eyes. "But I could use a little support now and then."

And there it was. The body blow. For all he'd tried to convince himself he'd kept his anger at her sickness to himself, he hadn't been fooling her. But his anger refused to surrender the helm.

"And what the hell do you mean by that? I do support you. I'm your husband. I pay the mortgage, I keep the money coming in. I put up with all the church stuff because I know you're struggling."

And now his turn: default bastard position. Turn the blame around. Good work, Nigel. You're one in a million.

She gaped at him. "Did I really hear that?" The tears slipped out and ran down her cheeks. "This is what I'm talking about. I'm alone in this marriage. You pay the bills, you come and go, but you… you never…" She seemed at a loss for words. "Damn it, Nigel – I'm not *contagious!*"

Here was the closest to passionate about their marriage he'd seen her in a long time. They were stripping the lies away, and although he had no idea where that would lead, for the first time in a while he felt as if he could almost breathe in his own home. His anger was starting to fade, overwhelmed by his own grimy guilt.

"Look," he said. "That's not what I meant." He paused. "I love you. You know that." True as it was, it sounded lame, even to him. "I just... I just find it difficult. I find the way it's changed you difficult. Can't you see that you've changed?"

Her shoulders slumped. "I don't know any other way to be. I can't go back to being the girl you dated. I was out of touch with myself then, out of touch with..." She hesitated, then seemed to push out the word. "...Him. I can't go back to being her. Too much has changed now – inside and out. And the things I've seen at the hospital. The dying. What *they* see. You should come with me and listen to them. Then maybe you'd understand better. He *comes* for them, Nigel, He really does. They see Him and it's beautiful."

He said nothing. He had enough problems dealing with the sickness at home. No way he could face a hospital.

After a moment she wiped her tears. "Do you want to leave?"

He stared at her, his stomach suddenly a gnarled mess of icy knots. Did he? Part of him wanted to turn tail and run. The easy way out. But could he leave her? That was the question. Because he did love her. Still. Under all that God crap, his Abby was still there. She had to be.

He loved her, but he'd stopped liking her. And the world was going to shit. Surely this was the time for them to stick together.

"Of course I don't want to leave." The anger was gone. "But I've got to go away tomorrow to interview someone about–" He caught himself from finishing the sentence with about how the plague started. They'd only go back round full circle. "About some stuff. Tying up a story. Maybe we both need to think about how we go on from here."

"Trust me, Nigel. That's all I think about these days." She sighed. "You finish spreading your little friends about. I'm going to bed."

He saw a moment as she brushed past him that he could have grabbed her and held her and hugged her close and told her they'd be all right, but that risked her pushing him away, and so he let it pass, and then she was heading out to the corridor and the stairs.

"I'll be up in a minute," he called after her.

Maybe a minute. Maybe an hour. Whenever she was asleep.

HENRY

"Do you see Him, love?"

Maggie lay on her side on the blanket, her voice a soft croak as she spoke to Livvy. If Maggie was pale, poor little Liv was almost transparent. Henry knelt beside his wife and daughter, helpless.

"Who?" said Liv, the single syllable a supreme effort, her voice a ghostly echo.

"God, love. They say He comes to you near the end."

The end…the words were a knife in his heart, but that was what he was looking at, wasn't it: the end of his family, the end of the two dearest people in his world.

The end of his world.

"Light," Liv whispered.

"You see a light? That's Him! He's come for you! The Lord's come to take you home!"

Not to *our* home, Henry thought.

When they'd come down with the plague, he hadn't dared take them to the hospital – not after what had happened in Brighton. Hospitals were doing nothing for the plague anyway except watching the sick die. And he couldn't keep them home where their nosy fucking biddy neighbors who didn't miss a trick would notice and talk. So they'd gone on the run, ending in this stifling little empty tool shed on an abandoned farm outside Ludgershall. The doors were tight and lots of spiders had silked the high corners and the windows. Moonlight through the grimy panes lit some of those webs now.

In the faint light he watched Liv where she lay on her back, her breaths so shallow. He could almost make out her blue eyes through her pale, frail closed lids. What was she seeing? Really. All this talk about God coming at the end to guide the dying to the next life… how could that be real?

And yet…so many people mentioned seeing Him in their last moments, there had to be some kind of truth behind it. Didn't there?

"Light," Liv repeated, the word barely audible.

And then she stopped breathing.

Henry froze, not breathing himself, waiting for a breath, just one more breath, but none came. He leaned over and pressed his ear to her thin, flat chest, strained to hear, but all lay silent within – no heartbeat, not a breath.

No…no, this couldn't be. Not his little Liv! Eight years on this Earth. Only eight. Not fair! Not enough! Not nearly enough!

He moaned and began pressing on her chest. He'd never learned CPR but this seemed like what he'd seen on the telly. But how hard to press? How–?

"No," he heard Maggie say. "She's not coming back. She's with Him now… in a better place."

He knew that…he knew it…and so he took his nearly weightless Livvy in his arms and rocked her back and forth until he heard Maggie sigh.

"Light…see it…coming for me. Hello, God."

And then she too stopped breathing.

Still holding Liv, Henry stared at his wife who, in turn, stared at the ceiling with unseeing eyes.

Hello, God? What about *Good-bye, Henry?* Was it so wonderful, what they saw in that last moment?

He closed Maggie's eyes, gathered her against him, and rocked both his darlings, an arm against the back of each head so it wouldn't loll. So limp, so *light.* After a while he couldn't bear the feel of their skin cooling against his touch, so he laid them back and arranged their remains side by side, on their backs, legs straight, hands folded across their chests.

Now the hard part.

He went out to the car and returned with the can of kerosene he'd brought along just for this purpose. He'd known when they'd left home how this was going to end. He began to sob as he poured it over their still forms, glad he had only moonlight to work by and couldn't see their faces too well. At least they were at peace, while he was anything but. At least he could see to it they stayed at peace. He wasn't about to let the flies turn them into maggot farms. The little fucks would not be hatching more flies from his darlings.

When the can was near empty, he backed away, leaving a wet trail to the door. Then he pulled the butane lighter from his pocket and dropped to a squat. He thumbed a flame to life but couldn't bring himself to ignite the spilled fuel.

And yet he knew he must.

Clenching his teeth, he maxed the flame and played it against the end of the wet trail until it caught. The blue-yellow flame slowly inched along the floor toward his darlings. He couldn't watch them burn so he backed outside and closed the door.

Originally he'd thought he'd turn his back and rush away, but he couldn't leave. He had to make sure they caught and burned. He was safe from flies in the dark hours, so he stood and watched the windows as they began to glow, brighter and brighter as the flames consumed the remains of his darlings.

Eventually the dried wood siding of the shed caught and he had to back away from the heat, but still he watched. Under normal circumstances he'd have worried about fire fighters showing up to battle the blaze, but circumstances were far from normal. A rural fire was no longer a major concern. And even if it were, firefighter ranks had been gutted by disease and desertion. No one would come.

Henry watched until the shed collapsed upon itself with a gush of flame and a swirling barrage of sparks.

Now he could leave.

He sobbed as he drove north, toward London. His brother lived in town and his mum was still in Cricklewood. If he could sneak through the army lines, he'd pay a visit, say his good-byes, and then… what?

Jump in the Thames, he supposed. He couldn't think of anything to live for, and he wasn't about the let the bloody flies get him.

NIGEL

A high-pitched drone dopplered past his ear. It didn't seem loud enough to have awakened him, so maybe he was already awake. Or maybe his subconscious had become attuned to the sound of a—

Fly?

Nigel jolted upright in bed and looked around in the dark just as it buzzed by his ear again.

"Shit! We've got a fly!"

He fumbled for the nightstand lamp and switched it on. Next to him, Abby rolled away from the light and buried her face into the pillow. Her muffled cry sounded like a demand for a turtledove or some such. Nigel was about to respond when a quick look around the room locked his voice.

Flies…dozens of them…zipping through the air or clinging to the sheers over the windows.

This could not be happening. Bottling his terror, he shook Abby.

"What?" she said, eyes still closed, voice dripping annoyance as she lifted her head.

"Flies. We've got flies. Lots of them."

She snapped up to sitting and looked around. "Dear God, you're right! But how could–?"

"I don't know. I mean, you're awake, right? You see them too, right?"

"Absolutely."

Shit. He'd been hoping this was some sort of nightmare.

"Did you leave a window open?"

"Of course not. And they're all netted anyway."

Right. Right. He vaguely remembered hearing a clank from downstairs as he was falling off – but had it been it real? He couldn't seem to put his brain in gear. Think! Christ, one bite and they were goners. He wore a T-shirt and boxer shorts and his clothes lay draped over a chair half a dozen feet away. Too far to go with so much exposed skin.

The bedclothes – sheets and a light summer blanket. He grabbed the blanket and began pulling it from the bed.

"What are you doing?" Abby said.

"You take the sheet, I'll take this. Wrap up. Don't let them get you."

Abby flopped back and pulled the sheet over her head. "This way is even better."

"We can't just lie here and let them take over the house!"

"Our wonderful spiders will get them."

"You know damn well they're nowhere near ready for that!"

"We'll wait."

Still mad at him from before, obviously. Well, she had a right to be, he guessed. Still, her attitude was pissing him off.

"We've got to get rid of them, Abby. Are you going to help or not?"

Draping the blanket over his head and wrapping it around his body, he slipped out of bed and made a beeline for his clothes. Behind him, he heard a bitter laugh.

"You look like that crazy priest from *Gunga Din*. No, you're Cornholio!"

"Not funny!"

"No, wait-wait! You look like Mother Theresa."

"Abby–"

She laughed louder. "You've found God!"

"Shit!"

He shrugged off the blanket and pulled on his wrinkled shirt. How could she joke about this? Almost as if she–

The epiphany made him stop and turn.

"You don't care, do you?"

She sat up and gave him a puzzled stare. "I do. But…"

He felt his patience fraying as he pulled on his pants and warily watched the flies buzz around the room. They seemed more confused than aggressive.

"But what?"

"I've decided I'm not going to be afraid anymore."

Was she crazy? "Abby – one bite and it's over."

She rose from the bed and stood calmly in her overlong T-shirt and elastic forearm sleeve. "Yep, so why spend our time in fear? And God must want us, Nigel."

"*What?*"

She gestured to the flies. "Look at them. We have a swarm in our bedroom – in a house that's as secure as the Crown Jewels! What does that tell you?"

He didn't have an answer for that, but he'd go for anything but what Abby was saying. And whatever the cause he had to get rid of them. But first to find how they were getting in and put a stop to it.

Replacing the blanket over his head, he ran for the stairs to the first floor. He'd stocked up on bug spray but had stored it in the laundry room off the kitchen. A long trek. If–

The stench hit him as he stepped onto the first floor.

"Christ!"

He flipped a light switch and recoiled at the swarm of flies in the living room. They seemed concentrated around the fireplace. Something there, on the andirons. He stepped closer and the carrion stench almost overwhelmed him. He flipped on a brighter light and flinched at sight of the rotting… *thing* in the hearth. A dead squirrel or large rat or – whatever the thing was, it squirmed with maggots.

Many of the newly hatched flies had alighted on the mantle. Close up now he could see their bodies were shorter than the plague flies.

Suddenly he felt like an idiot. Cowering under a blanket in his own home all because of–

"Fuck!"

"What?"

He turned. Abby stood on the stairs, holding her nose. He didn't know if from relief or chagrin or a combination of both, he couldn't help it – he started to laugh.

"Bloody fucking house flies, is what!"

"That stink!"

He laughed again. "I'm so goddamn smart! When we sealed the chimney last month we must've trapped something in there with some houseflies. It died, they laid eggs, and the leftovers dropped through the damper!"

Abby wasn't laughing. She kept her hand over her nose and mouth.

"Don't worry," he told her. "I'll use the log tongs and bag it up and get it out of here."

Still no response.

Then he knew – or thought he did.

"Don't tell me you're disappointed?"

"We could have been together," she said around her hand.

"We *are* together."

"I meant with Him."

"Oh, for fuck's sake–"

"We'd be happy." She turned and hurried back upstairs. "We aren't happy now, that's for damn sure!"

He stepped to the stairs and called up after her. "We're not special, Abby. Your God didn't send a special squadron of flies after us – that's what's really eating you, isn't it."

The bedroom door slammed.

She's lost it, he thought. Completely lost it.

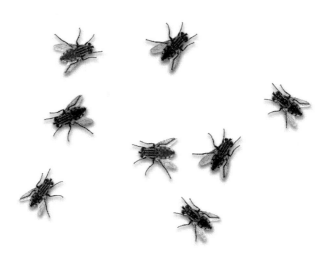

FRIDAY

BBC:

You are watching a live video feed from Beijing, a city that has become famous for its smog. But that's not smog you see hanging over the buildings. Those are flies. Apparently the death toll in the rural provinces has been staggering, with local authorities unable to bury the bodies. That in turn has led to an explosion in the fly population…

NIGEL

He'd almost hoped that Abby would still be in bed by the time he left the house but that wasn't to be. Their bedroom door had been shut when he'd crept out of the spare room and gone for a shower, but by the time he was out he could hear the kettle boiling downstairs.

Shit. His stomach knotted. The echo of their fight over dinner didn't bother him. That had faded to nothing compared to her revelation in the middle of the night. She didn't care if she got bitten because she'd be with God? What had happened to the woman he'd married?

"I'm making you eggs and bacon," she said, putting a mug of milky coffee on the breakfast bar for him. "I figure you're going straight to the paper?"

Nigel nodded. This wasn't quite the reception he'd been expecting. She wasn't looking him in the eye, but neither was she sulking or crying. The knot unfurled slightly. The problems between them hadn't gone away but it seemed neither of them was in the mood for confrontation this morning.

She pushed the bacon around in one pan, crisping the edges up, while eggs sizzled in a second. They smelled good.

"Nice breakfast."

"These sort of things won't keep so we might as well enjoy them while we can. The supplies in the shops are thinning out."

"It's going to work out, you know. They'll find a cure. They always do." He believed that. "But maybe we should think of stocking up on a few things."

She made a noncommittal noise.

He sipped his mug and was glad the small kitchen TV was on, burbling away in the background and filling the awkward silences. He hadn't been a fan when she'd decided she wanted one – he'd always thought having televisions in more than one room was the desperate act of couples who had nothing to say to each other anymore – but this morning he was grateful for it. And shit, maybe they *were* one of those couples now.

"I'm sorry we fought," he said, choosing his words carefully. This was a truce, not the end of the battle. "I was stressed and tired after the flight and work. I didn't want to fight with you."

"Me too." She reached for a couple of slices of bread and put them in the toaster. "And what I said last night?" She finally looked over at him. "I didn't mean I wanted to die. I'm not suicidal. I'm just not going to be afraid any more. Que sera, sera."

Here we go again.

"You know, Abby…" he kept his voice soft. He should have kept it silent but, just like her, he couldn't help himself when it came to speaking his mind. *That* was something they still had in common. "I can see how for someone with faith it would be easy to think that this whole plague is the work of some supreme being, but it isn't. This is butterflies-in-the-forest stuff."

He waited for her back to arch slightly with irritation, but it didn't.

Instead, she took a plate from the cupboard and started scooping out his eggs.

"Chaos theory," he said. Surely that would get a reaction. Was she even listening to him? At least she wasn't arguing back. "The wrong fly got caught in the wrong net and then got caught up in the wrong well-meaning project and something completely unpredictable happened. No one could have known what would happen. And if some lizard had then eaten that fly, none of this would have happened. The results had nothing to do with the Divine – just an unlucky chain of events. No one was even trying to–"

He frowned, his eye caught on the small screen. He recognized the photo of the face showing there. Rajiv Singh. What the hell was–?

"Can you turn that up?" he said.

"What?"

"The TV." Breakfast was forgotten as he pushed past her to get closer to the set. "Where's the damned remote?"

"Here. What's the matter with you?"

The irritation in her voice washed past him as he snatched the remote from her hand and turned up the volume.

The BBC breaking News red banner had a constant scroll running. *"British scientist, Rajiv Singh, identified as being the possible originator of the plague fly."*

"No, no, no…" he muttered.

How could they have this story? This was all his work and no one had seen it outside of the meeting at *The Light* yesterday. What the hell was going on?

"Oxford entomologist, Rajiv Singh, is one of the world's leading specialists in the study of insects and flies, according to sources who revealed this story today." The somber-faced female reporter was standing outside a three-story Georgian row house with all its curtains pulled closed. Was that Singh's house? Jesus. *"For three years, Dr. Singh ran a facility in Salonga National Park working on a project using gamma rays to sterilize the male tsetse fly."*

"What is it?" Abby said.

Behind him, the bacon still sizzled in the pan as the screen split to include the anchorman back in the studio.

"And this was in the Congo where the first plague cases were discovered?"

"Yes, that's right. Dr. Singh's research center closed down and six months afterward the first cases were reported barely more than five miles away. Of course, we can't be certain until we speak to Dr. Singh that his work there caused the plague to follow, but that's the logical conclusion."

"But that's not true!" Nigel's stomach turned to water. He turned to Abby. "We don't know that yet! We have no proof! It's all just circumstantial! And how the hell have they got my story? I've been holding it back until corroboration!"

"This is your–?" Abby started, but Nigel was already pushing past her.

She could wait. Her God could wait. He needed to get to *The Light* and get to the bottom of this clusterfuck before it all got out of hand.

Chaos theory, he thought again, as he stormed out of the front door, had a lot to fucking answer for.

ABBY

As the door closed behind Nigel, Abby drifted toward the TV to shut it off but paused, remote in hand, as the anchor switched to a "scientific expert." The man looked properly professorial with his wire-rimmed glasses and bow tie as his credits streamed across the bottom of the screen.

He blathered on about mutations, saying that the probability of Dr. Singh's gamma-ray sterilization of tsetse males inadvertently causing a significant mutation in another species of fly was remote. And that the probability of a single such mutation leading to this worldwide plague was even more remote. But under prompting by the anchor, he reluctantly admitted that, while highly improbable, it *was* possible.

That seemed to be what the anchor wanted to hear, because he immediately cut away to the outside Dr. Singh's home. It seemed that even in the minutes since Nigel had been watching, a crowd had gathered there – an angry crowd of ordinary people, jostling alongside the reporters and cameramen. A roving reporter had found a wild-haired Nigerian whose heavily accented English was difficult to decipher word for word, but the gist was clear: The white-man's plot to unleash a genocidal plague in Africa had backfired and now threatened the entire globe.

"Idiot," Abby muttered as she jabbed the remote's MUTE button. "Doctor Singh is Indian."

She turned to find the bacon burning. She switched off the heat. Ruined. No matter. Nigel was gone and she had no appetite.

She'd known from the start that he was angry about her lupus – angry that she'd come down with it. But when his anger had found no target, it turned on her renewed belief in God. And then it expanded to include her.

He seemed angry at everything now – the whole world.

Living together was becoming harder and harder but she had to stay with him. The Church forbade divorce. And besides, she rather suspected Nigel was another trial for her, an ongoing test of her faith.

Nigel…an instrument of the Lord. She found the irony fascinating.

She turned back to the silent screen and its view of the scene outside the researcher's house. As she watched, Nigel's words about chaos theory echoed through her brain.

Try as she might, she saw nothing truly chaotic about it. What had Jesus said? *And not one sparrow will fall to the ground without your Father's will.* Perhaps God had caused that mutation.

No…not perhaps. A certainty.

And why not? He worked in mysterious ways, often hiding His hand. For the key was faith, wasn't it. And if he showed His hand too blatantly, faith would no longer be necessary. Humanity would *know.*

Abby smiled. Yes, she liked that. Nigel hadn't been able to establish a link between Dr. Singh's work and the plague flies. To his credit, he was always rigorous in his search for truth – the whole truth. And he hadn't been satisfied that he'd found it, and so he'd held back the story.

But you'll never find the truth, Nigel, she thought. Because you're looking in the wrong place.

Thanks to Nigel, of all people, she saw how it had happened, how God had worked the string of cause and effect. A mutation in a fly's DNA altered a protein in its saliva that caused an autoimmune reaction in humans. God caused His latest creation to avoid the insectivores that might have ended its existence before it could breed, and He caused its first victim to miss when swatting at the little thing that had bitten him. God caused that DNA mutation to occur in a remote jungle so that the fly's untended dead victims could provide maggot fodder, leading to an explosion in the population of this new species… and thus a civilization-threatening plague.

A delicate daisy chain of cause and effect, all the way down the line, leading inexorably back to the Uncaused Cause: God.

Poor Nigel. Instead of shaking her faith, his rigorous research had only bolstered it.

But something else he'd said came back to her. Last night, during their fight, he'd said, *If you're such a fan of God's will, then why do you plug yourself into that machine every day? Why doesn't he save you?* It had niggled at her all night.

Because it was a good question. How could she, on one hand, argue for accepting God's will for the world, and then, on the other, subvert it when it came to the trial he'd sent her way?

A strange and sudden clarity suffused her. She'd sinned by falling away from God and the Church, and for that, an incurable illness had been visited upon her. The world too had fallen away from God and now it too faced an incurable illness.

The symmetry was as awesome as it was inescapable.

One way or another she was going to die at the hand of her Lord and God. She saw now that she'd been given a choice, and she had no doubt about her decision.

Feeling almost giddy, she turned off the TV and tossed the remote on the couch. Then she hurried upstairs to the master bath where she found Nigel's travel kit. She rummaged through it until she came up with his straight razor. He'd told her he carried it because he never knew when he'd need a shave in a place with no electricity. Plus it doubled as a handy cutting tool when he needed one.

She opened it and stared at the beveled blade.

Yes, this would do nicely.

Then she would go to the hospital. Her dialysis schedule and the fatigue of the lupus had made full-time nursing impossible. But she could still go in and comfort the sick and dying. That was the Lord's work, and this was her day to volunteer.

HENRY

Henry tore his gaze from the dark, earnest face on the TV screen. Dr. Rajiv Singh…

He nudged his brother in the chair next to him. "That's the fuck what killed my…" His vision blurred as the names clogged in his throat. He forced them through. "My Maggie and Liv."

"Where?"

He pointed to the screen. "There. Him."

But the face was gone, replaced by a view of the mob scene outside the fucker's home. A nice home. Better than anything Henry ever could have provided for his loved ones.

He never drank this early in the day and he'd already had too much for any time of day. But that didn't stop him from signaling for another whiskey to go with his Newkie. They'd run out of Guinness and didn't know if they'd be getting more in. He couldn't afford it, but so what? His life savings were tucked in his pocket, and he had nothing and no one left to save for.

"What are you talkin' about?" Jamie said.

His older brother was heavier with a red face and a veiny nose. This wasn't too early in the day for him. Not a bit.

"The guy who started the plague – that Indian cunt."

"Weren't no Indian," Jamie's friend Alex said. He'd gone prematurely gray and sported a short, salt-and-pepper beard. "Was the Chinese. They started with AIDS but that only got rid of the queers – and not enough of them, y'ask me. Then their bird flu didn't work out, so now they're trying this."

Had Henry known Alex better he would have told him straight off to shut his face, but he was Jamie's mate and so he kept quiet. But damn, the dickhead hadn't heard a conspiracy theory he didn't love.

"No, they're saying this scientist here x-rayed the flies that started the plague."

Alex made a sour face. "'They'? Who? The BBC? They only feed you what the government wants you to hear. And as for flies, they don't spread the plague. They're just a smokescreen. It's a virus. You catch it like you catch a cold. The only protection is vitamin E. Two thousand units a day'll do it. I take four."

Fucking idiot, Henry thought as he watched the screen.

But he had to admit Alex put his health where his mouth was. He'd arrived at the pub bareheaded in a short-sleeve shirt while Henry and Jamie had worn gloves and a couple of the beekeeper hats Jamie had snagged before there'd been a run on them.

Alex would catch the plague real soon. Because it wasn't contagious. Maggie and Liv had been bitten and they got sick; Henry hadn't been bitten and he'd tended his two loves through their last minutes and hadn't got sick.

He didn't trust the government any more than Alex, but his gut told him this wasn't – what did they call it? – misinformation? No. *Dis*information. This wasn't any of that. This sounded real. It accused a scientist connected to the government of causing the plague. Would the government blame itself? Not likely.

No…the flies brought the plague. And Dr. Rajiv Singh had made the flies.

The TV cameraman was scanning the crowd outside this Singh's house. They were all muffled against the haze of flies buzzing around them. Someone threw a rock. It sailed through the air and bounced off the front door.

In that instant Henry knew where he wanted to be – *needed* to be. He turned to his brother.

"You know where that is?"

Jamie squinted at the screen. "Somewhere in Camden, looks like. What d'you think Al?"

Alex nodded. "I'd say you're right."

Henry knocked back his whiskey and gulped the rest of his ale.

"Take me there," he said, rising.

The room wobbled a bit and he had to grab the edge of the stable to steady himself.

"What?" Jamie said. "Into that mob?"

Henry nodded. He craved a word or two with Dr. Rajiv Singh.

NIGEL

The wall of the first floor of the Singhs' terraced house had been whitewashed but the two upper levels were natural stone. Every window on all three floors was shattered. Nigel had fought his way through the crowd to the front door and the two policemen posted there.

Despite raising his ski mask – red with blue stripes, unlike the black balaclava style in vogue – to expose his face and showing his press credentials, they refused to let him pass. Nigel, in turn, refused to take no for an answer.

"But Doctor Singh will *want* to speak to me," he said. "I may be the one man able to clear up some of this misunderstanding."

This morning he'd arrived at *The Light* and couldn't find his thumb drive. He'd turned his office upside down but it was gone. No one had duplicated his research – they'd stolen it. Must have hacked through his password too.

He'd called the entomologist at the museum but he hadn't come in today. Nigel hoped to hell he hadn't caught the plague. He'd headed toward Sussex but had been turned back. His press credentials had been no more useful there than here.

"Look, sir," one of the officers finally said, "I've got no doubt you're exactly who you say you are, but even if the folks inside wanted to talk to you – and they don't want to talk to *anybody* from the press – we can't let anyone in. You can understand that." He gestured behind Nigel. "I let you in and they'll want in too."

Nigel turned and looked. The crowd filled the street from pavement to pavement and corner to corner. Somewhere behind the threatening rain clouds the sun had dropped below the horizon. Darkness was falling, but instead of dispersing, the crowd seemed to be growing. The flies stopped swarming at night and that would perhaps bring even more people outside.

"They're already ugly," said the other constable. "Been picking cobblestones out of the road and flinging them at the house. A little spark and we could have a full-scale riot on our hands. And letting you inside could just be that spark. So why don't you do us all a favor and move on."

Nigel's impulse was to keep pushing, but he saw the way some of those at the front were glowering at him and decided on discretion.

He turned back to the policemen. "Okay. We'll do it your way. But if you think you're sitting on such a tinderbox, why not just get the Singhs out of here?"

The bobbies exchanged a weary glance.

The first said, "That's in the works."

"Been in the works all day," said the second.

Down at the end of the block, he saw a TV truck with a dish on top. A cameraman stood on the roof, recording the scene. Nigel headed that way. He knew a fair number of TV people. Maybe they could help him.

THE WHITTINGTON HOSPITAL

Funny how things changed, Dr. Kumaran thought, and so quickly.

He sipped bad coffee from the machine and waited for the volunteer nurse, Abby, to join him for what had become their habitual daily rounds. At first, after the flies had hit London, no one in the hospital wanted to walk amongst the dying. They did, of course. That was their job, and they knew – at least the rational part of their minds knew – that the plague was terrible and deadly, but it wasn't contagious. Still, to watch it ravage a body so quickly when you could do nothing to help was entirely against the nature of those who had trained so hard to heal.

When it had started, and the first wave of victims had flowed in, Manu Kumaran had been reminded of the early days when he practiced medicine in the slums of Mumbai. Endless sickness that couldn't be held back however much you tried. He'd learned that lesson quickly. Poverty would always win, as would disease. Every life saved was nothing compared to the masses who were dying. The battle would be relentless and unwinnable.

Now, the civilized world was learning first hand that same lesson from thirty years ago. The flies would win. He'd known that from the first news reports. He'd felt it in his water, as some of the old boys in the geriatric ward would say. Some not so much older than him, he had to admit, and his water held less well than it had back in the sticky heat of India.

But still, when he'd seen humanity's end coming, he did what he'd done all those years ago: drawn his squat frame tall and vowed at least to ease the suffering of those whose paths he crossed. Kindness, that was the best medicine he had to offer – something very much forgotten in the overworked and underpaid corridors of so many NHS hospitals where quotas and budgets and staffing crises overtook such ethereal qualities.

Despite being a heart specialist, he had taken to visiting the sick, the ones without family at their bedside, and talking softly to them, holding their hands and listening to their fears and thoughts before the disease bore them off. So many had no other visitor. Another lesson few learned until too late was that fear would so often win out over love. Governments across the world could scream out that this deathly plague wasn't contagious, but who trusted governments anymore?

Now, however, it would seem as if, in their very dying, the ill-fated patients had some kindness of their own to give back.

"Shall we?"

The voice was soft and, without looking to his side, Dr. Kumaran nodded.

He hadn't known the young volunteer until he had found her sitting among the dying one night, her eyes wide in wonder, talking soothingly as she held onto a middle-aged man's hand. But the man had been comforting her, not the other way round, even if he had been so unaware.

Yes, Kumaran thought as he started to walk, strange how things change.

"Do you believe it's really God they see?" she asked.

For a moment Dr. Kumaran wasn't sure how to answer. Did he think that? Were these beautiful, joyous visions the dying experienced really a message from a supernatural being? Or were they just a byproduct of the failing organs, nature providing an accidental kindness of her own in the moments before expiration? Hypoxia? A serotonin release? Dopamine?

Even as a child he'd had no truck with religion of any form. Chemicals and cells, that was all humanity was – all crystal clear to him, and he'd never felt any loss for a lack of faith. But recently, on these quiet, private night walks when his shifts were done, he had found himself beginning to wonder. The hallucinations – the visions – were all so similar. The descriptions were all so passionate and glorious that he could not stop a seed of doubt from entering his mind.

No, for himself, he had no real answer yet. He found peace of sorts from watching the last moments of the dying, but were they seeing God? He hoped never to learn the answer to that question.

"All that matters," he said, as they opened the ward door and stepped inside, "is whether you think it is God."

"I do," she said, nodding with an enviable certainty.

He surveyed the daunting scene before him: private rooms with two or three beds and cots, semi-private rooms crammed with four or more, gurneys and cots in the hallways. So many. Too many.

But he managed a smile as he watched Nurse Abby move among them like a wraith, a soothing presence, bringing peace and acceptance. She stopped at a young woman's bedside and took her hand. Several of the patients were becoming agitated. The visions were coming. He let peace settle in his soul.

HENRY

They'd been passing a bottle of dark rum back and forth during the tube ride to Camden, and by the time they arrived Henry was thoroughly bladdered. They wandered around a bit until they found the crowd. Wasn't hard. Couldn't miss it. Huge.

Henry didn't let that stop him. He barged right in, weaving an unsteady path among its members in their long pants and long sleeves – turtlenecks had made a big comeback – and gloves despite the summer heat.

"Where can I get one of those?" a man said, pointing to Henry's veiled bee helmet.

The man wore one of those patterned Arab scarves wrapped around his head and face, although the small areas of pale skin visible around his goggles said he was from a lot farther north than the Mid East. Looked like a Norwegian Arafat. A lot of people in the crowd wearing those Arab things. Had to be hot under them. Even though the light breeze was heavy and humid with crowd sweat, at least the mesh veil on Henry and Jamie's helmets let it through.

"You don't need none of that," said Alex, pointing to the surgical mask over his mouth and nose as he brought up the rear of their trio. "Just this."

Still insisting that the flies didn't carry the plague, the only thing he'd added to his outfit upon leaving the pub was the mask. The guy in the Arab scarf stepped back at sight of Alex and all his exposed flesh. A normal reaction, Henry guessed, when confronted with madness.

They moved on, careful not to trip in the gaps left by pried-up cobblestones. The nearer the house, the tougher the going until Henry got the bright idea of putting Alex in the lead. People made way for him.

When they finally reached the house, Henry saw two ruddy-faced policemen stationed at the front door. But no lights on inside, despite the deepening dusk.

"I'll bet they're not even home," Henry said, disappointed.

"Oh, they'll be home all right," said a muffled woman's voice directly to his left.

She had an Irish accent but was dressed in one of those dark blue thingies that cover Arab women from head to toe. Henry knew the name... burrr... burka. This one even had netting over the eyeholes. Perfect for fly protection. Maybe those Islamic nutters weren't so daft after all.

"Yeah, we spied himself earlier," said the big man next to her in an even thicker accent. "Peekin' out the window, he was."

Henry stared at the lifeless house. "Well, then they've run off out the back since then."

"Oh, they tried," said the woman, "but people out in their rear garden started throwin' stones at 'em. Drove 'em back inside."

"Good," Henry said. He eyed the front door, painted a stark black against the white wall. "I've got a bone to pick with him."

"Don't we all," said the man. "But you can forget that. Those coppers aren't letting anyone near the door."

Henry could see that. A wasted trip. He'd wanted to look that heathen bastard in the eye and ask him why he'd fucked up those flies so they killed his Maggie and Liv.

"Now what?" Jamie said.

"We wait." Henry folded his arms. "Gotta come out some time."

Swaying, Alex turned to them and whispered, "We can charge those coppers. Three of us and two of them."

The idea had merit, and Henry was considering it when he was distracted by a bit of light blurring through the air. At first he thought it might have been a figment of the rum, but then it crashed through an already broken first-floor window and exploded inside. Flames blossomed and lit the darkness within.

Henry cried, "Was that a–?"

"Yeah-yeah," said the big Irishman. "A feckin' Molotov cocktail!"

While the coppers gaped, another bottle flew through a second-floor window and belched flame into the evening air.

As smoke began to pour from the shattered windows, the policemen rushed up and banged on the door – to evacuate the family, no doubt. A hail of cobblestones replaced the cocktails. Most banged and thudded off the walls, but enough connected with the pair to knock them flat.

Just then the black door opened and a man appeared with a woman and a little girl, all backlit by the flames behind them.

"That's him!" Henry screamed. "That's the fucker!"

At sight of them a cry went up from the mob. The rum haze Henry had been moving through vaporized in a blast of rage. Everything became agonizingly, heartbreakingly clear. Maggie and Livvy were dead and this man had killed them, just as sure as he'd put a bullet through each of their heads.

He dropped to a knee and clawed at the cobblestones, already loosened by others before him. Got his fingers around one, reared back, and let it fly without aiming. It bounced harmlessly off the wall. But he wasn't alone in the task. More stones flew from elsewhere in the crowd, driving the Singhs back into their burning home.

"Burn!" Henry screamed. "Burn in hell!"

They'd closed their door against the hail of rocks. They couldn't stay in there. They–

"The back!" he said. "That's where they're going!"

The big Irish guy had said some of the crowd was out back in the garden. Would they let them out? Damn fuck better not. He was about to fight his way toward the end of the block to reach the rear when he noticed movement at the first floor window to the right of the door.

Silhouetted against the flames inside, someone was raising the sash. It made no sense – all the panes were broken anyway. But as a small form was lowered through the opening, Henry understood – the Singhs were trying to sneak their daughter out of the house.

The sight of it triggered memories of Livvy's body being consumed by flame, and something detonated inside Henry.

"No way! No fucking way!"

He ran forward, grabbed the child, and hurled her back through the window. If his daughter had to burn, so did Singh's.

An explosion shook the house and even the street, blasting billows of flame from the first-floor windows. Henry saw the little girl thrown against the sill, engulfed in flame, and then she toppled back inside.

Henry backed away, stumbling as he stared in horror at the window, empty but for the flames that roared from it.

What had he just done? What in God's name had he *done*?

NIGEL

With a conscious effort, Nigel shut his gaping jaw. But as much as he wanted to look away from the monitor, he could not.

Seconds ago he'd been joking with a producer he'd known for years. And then the first Molotov had hit. All eyes had turned to the monitors carrying the feed from the roof of the truck. Conversation ebbed with the second, and died when the Singhs were refused egress from their front door.

With the final atrocity – hurling that poor child back through the window – the interior of the truck had gone dead silent. For a few seconds, no one moved, no one even breathed. And then cries and moans and profanities filled the air. Nigel stayed silent. He had no choice. His tongue seemed to weigh a ton and his mouth was dry as the Sahara.

The Singhs…an entire family… father, mother, child… gone… all gone.

Many people, in the mob and in the media, had contributed to the atrocity he'd just witnessed. The police too – yes, they were short-handed with more and more failing to show up for work, choosing to stay at home rather than expose themselves to the plague – but it had been obvious even to a casual observer that the situation outside the Singh house had been a powder keg.

But what could be obvious to only one man was that it had all started with the carelessness of one man.

Me, Nigel thought. This horror began with me.

ABBY

Nigel pulled off his striped ski mask as he stepped through the door and looked exactly like she knew he would. And she knew why. The telly had been replaying the horrific scene nonstop. Her heart went out to him.

"Nigel, you can't blame yourself."

He looked surprised to see her. "Tell me who else I can blame and I'll do so. With relish."

"It's not as if you published that story."

"No, but my notes and research were used to set a match to that poor man and his family. Even if they were stolen–"

"Stolen? Oh, no."

He nodded. "Oh, yes. Someone stole my thumb drive and sold it to a BBC stringer. I hope he chokes on the money."

"Well, there, you see? You can't be–"

"Abby, I was there!" He dropped onto the couch and buried his face in his hands. "I watched that little girl... if I'd just stuck that drive in my pocket before leaving the office, she'd still be..."

Was that a sob? She'd never heard Nigel cry. He could be such a cold, obstinate bastard at times, and those times had become more and more frequent lately. But she knew another Nigel, one who felt deeply.

There – another sob. The pure anguish in the sound drew her to his side like iron to a magnet. She reached out, hesitated – how would he react? – then laid her hand on his shoulder.

"Oh, Nigel, it's all right."

He dropped his hands from his face and covered her hand with one of his.

"No, it's not. But thank you for saying that." He shot to his feet. "I need a drink."

"Are you sure that's a good idea?"

"It'll be the best thing that's happened to me all day."

Well, she guessed she could use some wine herself.

"I've got more of that red."

"I need something a little harder. I have a bottle of Irish I've been saving, and this just might be the night for it."

She hadn't known about that. "Where is it? I'll–"

"I stashed it in the desk," he said, walking toward the dialysis room.

A minute later he emerged with a bottle, his straight razor, and a concerned expression.

"I found this in there."

Crap. Think!

"I needed it to open something."

"We have every sort of knife in the next room."

The truth burst from her like vomit. "I was going to cut up and empty all the dialysate bags."

He put the bottle on the table and looked like she'd just slapped him across the face.

"What? Why on Earth...?"

She forced a shrug. "I got to thinking about what you said last night and had to agree: If putting spiders around the house was thwarting God's will, so was dialysis five times a week."

He took a step closer. "Have you gone *completely* crazy? That… that's insane!"

"You know the saying, 'Let go, let God?'"

"Yeah – it means let go of all responsibility for yourself." He stared into her eyes. "I know I can be a selfish shit, but am I that bad to live with? You'd rather die than go on living with me?"

"Why does it always have to be about you, Nigel? This was between me and God."

"What? Did you have a conference call? A little tête-à-tête while I was out?"

"Don't start."

"Really? Because last time I looked, suicides went straight to hell."

"I didn't see it that way at first. I thought I was putting myself in God's hands and letting him decide whether I live or die."

"You could play Russian roulette and say the same thing! At least then you've got a five-in-six chance of survival. But stopping dialysis leaves you *zero* chance. You know and I know, Abby, that without regular use of that machine in there, you're a goner!"

She couldn't argue that.

"Wouldn't have worked anyway," he added, "because I'd have carted you straight to the hospital."

"I wouldn't have gone."

"You damn well would have, even if I had to carry you!"

"I'd refuse treatment."

"I'd tell them you've gone 'round the bend!"

"You'd have to prove that, and you couldn't. And really, Nigel, don't you think they've got their hands too full with plague victims to waste time on a perfectly healthy-looking woman who wants nothing to do with them?" She shrugged again. "But it's all moot because I couldn't do it."

He took another step toward her. "What changed your mind?"

"If it isn't suicide, it's close to suicide. I wasn't just letting go and letting God, I was actively destroying something that my life depended on."

'Jesus,' he said.

She let the word go this time. For the first time in a long while, she could see something close to love for her in his expression.

"I'm glad you saw the light." He took her hands in his. "You frighten me, Abby."

The tension between them vanished. It was good to feel him touching her – wanting to touch her – even if it was something as simple as holding hands.

"I frighten myself sometimes," she said. "Especially this morning. When I made the decision I had such clarity, such *peace*. But when I went to do it a voice inside me screamed, '*Stop!*' And I looked down at the razor and asked myself what was wrong with me. Is the lupus affecting my brain? I dropped the razor and ran from the room. I went to the hospital and helped people die of the plague. Somehow that made more sense."

"What's happened to you, Abby?" His voice choked. "Where did you go? I want you back."

She took him in her arms and didn't say what she thought: Your old Abby is gone for good. They simply held each other.

When he'd found the razor she expected anger, rage that she'd even considered stopping dialysis. She hadn't been prepared for his grief.

SATURDAY

CANINE GENOCIDE?

LONDON – Veterinary clinics have reported a massive upsurge in requests to euthanize the family dog. People from all walks of life, from bank clerks to pensioners, are bringing their beloved pooches to the vet and requesting they be put down in as peaceful and painless a manner as possible. They request the act remain a secret from the rest of the family, preferring to tell their spouses or children that the dog ran away and has never returned. The truth of the matter is that they can no longer risk the twice- or thrice-daily routine of taking the dog for a walk. The plague flies have transformed a pleasant outing for the pet into a death-defying exploit for the owner. Those who have a garden, and can simply open the door and let the animal out, have no problem. But it's an entirely different story for apartment dwellers. The number of dogs found dead of rat poison in public rubbish bins indicates that some owners prefer a do-it-yourself approach. (The Guardian)

NIGEL

Mal stood over Nigel's desk, shaking his head. "You look like pure, unadulterated shit."

Nigel didn't look up. His head felt ready to explode and he was sure if he moved it too fast it would split off and topple onto his desk.

"If only I felt that good."

"The Singhs?"

"Among other things, but they headed the list."

He'd put a major dent in the bottle of Midleton last night, but it hadn't helped then, and it had only hurt this morning. He hadn't been completely straight with Mal. Abby had replaced the Singhs as his number-one cause of grief. The fact that she'd even considered committing slow suicide like that – unbelievable. They stayed up awhile, just holding each other, then she'd gone to bed and he'd stayed with the Midleton.

Mal sighed. "Remember the other night at the pub when I said I thought you'd had enough plague for a while?"

"Vaguely."

"Well, I no longer think it, I *know* it."

Nigel raised his head – carefully – and looked at him. "Oh, no. Oh, no."

"We've already had this conversation."

"I said after I got back from Sussex–"

"Which you are."

"But I didn't get *into* Sussex."

"Doesn't matter. You're off the plague. I thought you looked wrecked before, but you're even worse now."

"You think I don't have reason?"

"That's my point: You have *too much* reason. You need something closer to the ground."

The conversation was coming back to him now. "That missing child you mentioned?"

"Right. My wife's cousin's little boy – Bandora."

"Pandora?"

"No. Bandora, with a B as in *boy*. His parents are from Burundi and it's a Kirundian name."

"They're Africans?"

Mal nodded. "Been here almost a year now. They're both Tutsis whose own parents were driven out of Rawanda by the Hutu attacks.

They settled in Burundi. My wife might have been born in South London but her family roots go back there."

"And the boy?"

"He's two years old and–"

"Two? Well he sure as hell didn't walk away, did he."

"No. That's my point. No one saw him abducted, but that's got to be it."

"No ransom demand?"

"None. He's been missing for over a week now and no word from anyone. The police are too tied up with plague to devote any attention to finding him. If there'd been a ransom demand, they might have acted, but I doubt it. His mother, of course, is inconsolable."

As any parent would be. And the lack of police response was becoming a more and more common complaint. But with anarchy growing – he cringed at the memory of the scene outside the Singh house – and their ranks progressively thinned by desertion and disease... what could people expect?

"And you think I can find him?"

"I hope so. You've got a knack for that sort of thing."

"A lot of good it did Rajiv Singh."

"This is different."

"You know the odds of finding him alive after seventy-two hours, don't you?"

Mal closed his eyes and nodded. "I know. But there's a story here, Nigel. I feel it deep in my bones. With all that's going on, someone steals a child. Why?"

"Pervs don't think like we do. The outside world doesn't work on them like it does us. The internal world of their fucked-up obsession is in the driver seat." He snapped his fingers as a thought struck. "You said his folks are Tutsis. Could this be a Hutu thing?"

He remembered Hutus killing something like 800,000 Tutsis in Rawanda back in the 90s. Why not?

"That was a systematic genocide. If this were Hutu-on-Tutsi violence, they would have entered the home and slaughtered them all with machetes. We've got something entirely other here."

"Just a thought."

Mal smiled. "You're thinking about it, at least. A good sign. Let's go. I'll introduce you to the parents and you can get started."

"Where?"

"Harrow."

Nigel groaned and tried to think of something he wanted to do less. Failed. Yesterday had left him physically and emotionally knackered, but delving into this little mystery might provide some sort of distraction. God knew he needed one.

Right. *God*…the guiding hand behind all this. At least according to Abby.

—————

"What are their names again?" Nigel said as Mal guided his Mondeo into a parking space on a residential street.

The drive had been uneventful but depressing as they'd headed north out of the center of the city. Although Harrow was only ten miles or so, not so long ago the journey would have taken the best part of an hour. The congestion charge had been introduced under the guise of reducing the traffic but was in fact just more revenue in government coffers; the flies had done more to clear the streets of traffic than it ever could.

The healthy work force, what was left of it, was being encouraged to work from home where possible. And in this awful heat if you had no air-con in your car you'd be royally screwed after a few minutes without opening a window. And no one drove in London with their windows open anymore. No one sane, at any rate.

Thankfully, Mal's car was top of the range. The cool air hadn't helped the chill Nigel had felt as they'd driven through the streets of Harrow. They passed a closed-down secondary school. The broken windows and bright graffiti adorning its walls proclaiming exactly what the ex-students thought of the place and several of its teachers. He couldn't help but wonder how many of them were dead now. The plague wasn't limiting itself to the inner city. It had reached Harrow too, and the numbers were rising.

"Gahiji and Uwimana Hakizimana."

"Quite a mouthful."

"Bantu-derived names tend to be long and usually mean

something, though I don't have the faintest what."

They pulled on their gloves and ski masks and got out of the car.

Nigel couldn't help a bitter laugh. "Look at us. Times have really changed, haven't they. Just a few months ago we'd have been suspected of being assassins or, at the very least, up to no good."

"Right. Now we're just two blokes out in daylight."

Mal led him up the walk to a two-story detached house with a brick front and bay windows on both floors. The place had to be worth nearly half a million quid.

"Wait. I got the impression they were refugees or something."

Mal shook his head. "Uwimana – the mother – is a well-respected artist. Her paintings go for good money. They said they wanted to get away from all the tribal politics back home."

He rang the bell and they waited. And waited. More ringing and knocking but still no answer.

"Should have called ahead, I suppose," Nigel said.

Mal frowned. "I didn't think it necessary. Uwimana told my wife one of them always stayed home because they were afraid to leave the phone unattended, in case somebody called."

"Maybe someone did."

"Maybe."

He twisted the knob. It turned.

Nigel said, "Uh-oh. I've seen this movie."

Mal nodded. "Me too. Maybe we'd better call the police."

"Maybe. But first…"

Nigel walked over to the attached single-car garage. The wooden swing-up door was painted white to match the rest of the trim. He bent and tugged on the handle. The door angled up, revealing a dark blue 7-series BMW.

Mal came up beside him.

"Bugger."

Nigel had to admit his curiosity was piqued. No, more than that – his antennae were quivering with alarm. Something going on here.

"Before we make that call, maybe you should stick your head inside and announce yourself. Just in case."

Mal nodded. "Right then."

Back at the door, Mal pushed it open, revealing a rather opulently furnished living room, and leaned across the threshold.

"Uwimana? Gahiji? It's Mal – Malcolm Brown. Are you home?"

Nigel sniffed the warm, stale air flowing from within. It stank of... something. These folks were from equatorial Africa, so he could imagine them leaving their air-con off, but not with this stench.

"What's that smell?"

Mal sniffed. "Something's rotten..."

"...in the borough of Harrow."

Not a carrion odor, though. And the living room looked fairly neat. Through an arch at the rear of the room he could see part of a formal dining room with the chairs all neatly arranged around a mahogany table.

"Looks all right," Mal said, "but time to make that call, I think. I left my phone in the car."

All Nigel's story instincts were pushing against his back, trying to propel him through that door, but Mal had the lead here. He had just pulled his phone free of his pocket when Mal grabbed his arm.

"Wait. You hear that?"

"What?"

"Something thumped above the ceiling. Listen."

Nigel strained to hear but the house was deathly silent.

"I get nothing."

He began to dial but Mal grabbed his arm again. "I know I heard something. Let's take a look."

Nigel suppressed a fist pump. Thought you'd never ask.

Mal stepped inside, repeating his call-out. Still no answer. He pulled off his ski mask as he moved farther in. Nigel did the same. No use in terrifying anyone who might be here.

The living room and dining room were indeed neat and clean, but the kitchen...

Mal made a face. "There's the rot."

The contrast to the first two rooms was jarring. Dishes were heaped in the sink, a plastic rubbish bin overflowed, and take-away containers and spoiled food littered every horizontal surface.

"Place is a shambles," Nigel said. "Looks like they've done nothing but order in. I know you said they didn't want to leave the house, but–"

Mal headed for the stairs. "The sound came from the second floor, I'm sure of it."

Nigel followed him up. The first bedroom they saw was obviously a child's – empty – with guardrails on the sides of the single twin bed. The second was furnished as an office with a desk and computer and bookshelves. At the end of the hall – double doors, closed.

"There," Mal said, pointing. "That's right over the front room where I heard the noise."

He stepped to the doors and knocked on the right one.

"Uwimana? Gahiji? It's Malcolm Brown."

A faint, raspy voice, barely audible, seeped between the doors.

"I'm coming in," Mal said.

Nigel held his breath as Mal tugged the door open. No telling what they were walking into. Visions of tribal violence, blood-spattered walls, severed limbs, unimaginable carnage flickered against the back wall of his brain.

Instead, he saw a frail black couple sprawled on a filthy bed in a miasma of urine and feces.

"Dear God!" Mal said, inching forward.

"Are they…?"

Nigel held back. His stomach, already fragile from the hangover, threatened to add to the mess they'd walked into.

"Uwimana! Gahiji! What's–?"

The man lifted a forearm and the woman spoke in a whisper. "Zahran."

Mal whirled, eyes wide. "They've got the plague!"

Nigel still had his phone in his hand. "I'll call it in. What's the street address?"

After Mal told him, he punched in 999 and made the report. The woman he spoke to promised to send an ambulance "as soon as possible." When he asked how long that would be, she repeated the phrase.

With the way things were, Nigel wondered if that even meant today.

Mal had moved to the bedside. "We've called for help. How long have you been sick?"

The man held up three fingers.

Mal glanced at Nigel with little hope in his eyes. Plague victims rarely last past the third day. Obviously too weak to get to the bathroom, they'd soiled their bed.

"Such foolish mistake," the man said in a voice like a tree limb brushing a wall.

"What was?"

"Such price to pay," was all he said.

"We called for help."

The man gave a feeble wave. "Nooooo. We do not deserve."

"Of course you do. We came to help find Bandora."

The woman had looked comatose but she jerked at the sound of the name. "Bandoraaaaa," she sobbed. "Zahraaaan."

"What does Zahran mean?" Nigel whispered. He didn't know why he whispered; maybe because their voices were so weak.

Mal shrugged. "Haven't a clue."

He tried to get more out of them but the man kept saying "We do not deserve" and the woman seemed limited to repeating, "Bandoraaaaa… Zahraaaan."

Nigel glanced around the room, wanting nothing more than to flee the stench. He went to one of the windows and pulled up the shade. The screen beyond the glass looked intact – no holes. He pulled up the sash to let in some air. He did the same on the other side. The hot breeze helped clear the stink some.

He looked away from the two dying people on the bed. Unless Abby's mythical God Himself intervened, it appeared Bandora would soon be an orphan. All the more reason to find him.

Nigel looked around. An array of paintings with lots of bright colors, especially red, decorated the walls. The wife's artwork? He wandered to the dresser and saw two framed pictures of the parents – in one they dressed in traditional flowing African garb, in the other they wore more formal European attire.

But no photos of their child.

"Ask them if they've got a picture of the boy," he said.

Mal did so and was rewarded with a "Bandoraaaaa" from the woman and racking sobs from the man. After a last look around, Nigel slipped out into the hall and went hunting. First stop: the child's room.

Nothing special there. A collection of what he supposed were typical toddler toys – never having had a child, he couldn't say for sure, but they seemed about right. No baby photos in sight, but…

On the wall, a charcoal sketch of a small child.

Could that be him? Well, who else would it be? It looked like something done by one of those itinerant sketch artists who dot the London parks, but probably done by his mother.

Mal came in behind him. "I tried to give them water but Gahiji's getting agitated. And the more I tell him help's on the way, the more – here, what's that now?"

"Bandora, I assume. This look like him?"

Mal shook his head. "Never seen him."

"I got the impression you knew–"

"They've never been very social, and always very protective of Bandora – almost obsessive about it. We thought perhaps he was disabled or had a learning disability of some sort." He frowned. "In fact, I don't think we ever saw Uwimana and Gahiji together."

"If they're with him all the time, then how in bloody hell did someone make off with him?"

"Good question." He jerked a thumb back toward the master bedroom. "But I don't think a detailed answer will be forthcoming anytime soon, if ever."

"Why no photos?"

"I've heard some primitive East African people believe a camera can steal your soul."

"Well, his parents don't look primitive and they weren't camera shy, so–"

"I told you: They were very protective of their child. Maybe–"

They both jumped at the sound of a gunshot.

"Christ!" Mal cried. "The bedroom!"

As he lurched toward the door, Nigel grabbed his arm. "Not so fast. The plague may have made him lose his mind. He may not recognize you."

Mal nodded. "Right, right."

Hurrying down the hall, they kept close against the right wall, out of the bed's line of sight. When they reached the double doors, Mal peeked through and then slammed back against the wall.

"Jesus cunting Christ!"

Nigel sneaked a look. His throat locked.

Uwimana lay flat on her back, just as they'd left her, except the front of her nightgown was soaked with pale blood. Gahiji sat propped up next to her with a revolver pressed against the middle of his throat, high up under his jaw.

"We should not see God," he rasped, and pulled the trigger.

His head flew back as the blast splattered blood and brains all over the wall behind him. Nigel felt his knees turn to water and he would have gone down had Mal not grabbed him.

"What the fuck!" Mal kept saying. "What the fuck!"

Nigel looked away and caught sight of one of the windows. Something was blocking the light. No, not something – *many* some-things. The screen was crawling with flies.

ABBY

Abby hadn't been surprised to find Nigel gone by the time she got up, and not surprised by her own relief at that fact. Last night she'd promised to keep up the dialysis and she meant to keep that promise. But another way of letting go and letting God had occurred to her as she'd fallen off to sleep. So simple. Why hadn't she seen it before?

As a result she'd had the best night sleep since her lupus diagnosis and she'd woken feeling rested and with a sense of both calm and purpose. She knew exactly what she had to do today, almost as if angels had whispered to her while she dreamed. Perhaps they had.

Nigel would see what she was doing as relinquishing all responsibility and giving up, not realizing that placing yourself truly in the hands of the Lord was taking the ultimate responsibility.

She made a cup of tea and used the last of the bacon for a sandwich. The fridge was nearly empty but they had a fair number of tins in the cupboards.

She didn't bother with a shower but dressed simply in cut-off denim shorts and a sleeveless T-shirt, and then dug her flip-flips out from under all her more protective footwear.

She was almost laughing as she grabbed her keys and wallet and headed out the front door. So good to have her skin free of layers of clothes, and when the outside warmth touched it she almost shivered with pleasure. She felt free at last. She felt perfect. She felt human. Strangely, she felt entirely alive.

The pavements were nearly empty, the oppressive heat too much for those still around to wander about covered in protective clothing. The few people she passed, wrapped up in the fear of their own mortality, pulled away from her, as if she was mad. She smiled at them though. She couldn't help it. Her hair felt good in the sunshine and as she moved through the streets she thought London had never looked so beautiful.

She went through the back alleys around Upper Street first, hoping to find success among the large wheelie bins where the restaurants would dump their waste, but was disappointed. Trade had died and so had supplies, and the managers had become far tighter on hygiene, leaving nothing overflowing or rotting to be found. She walked to King's Cross, smiling at the women who still loitered at various corners in states of undress, now armed with cans of fly-killer rather than mace. They didn't smile back, instead viewing her with suspicion and menace, as if she was a fresh rival for whatever little trade was left.

Abby didn't judge them. They would all be judged soon enough and by one far kinder and more understanding than she. She wanted to tell them to stop being afraid. She wanted to tell them a lot of things. Perhaps, if she got the chance, she'd come back and do just that. Spread the word.

She strolled down toward Baker Street and then wandered into Regent's Park, heading toward the lake at the heart of it. The weather was heavy and midges buzzed round her head. They tickled but she didn't swat them away. They were nature. They were His work, and all that aside it just felt good to be so unprotected that they could irritate her.

She had the park to herself. The pretty park cafe was closed. She wasn't surprised. Dogs were being put down or abandoned because no one wanted to walk them anymore and romantic strolls in the park were a thing of the past. For a while she'd heard talk of rapes and attacks on those who still tried to maintain a normal routine, but now the rapists were either dead or didn't think sex was worth exposing themselves to the plague. Abby felt as if she was the last person on earth.

For a while she lay on the grass and dozed contentedly, and when she finally sat up she checked her arms and legs but could find no sign of bites. Eventually she walked home, taking her time, waiting for God to find her if He so chose.

She paused at Mange Tout and bought a flat white to take away even though the mugginess in the air was getting heavier and she didn't really want it. She drank it anyway, her thoughts clouding with the sky. She'd come out this morning with such certainty at how the day was going to pan out that now she couldn't help feeling a slight sense of confusion and despondency. Perhaps He had not yet decided on her path. The caffeine rush on her empty stomach triggered a small wave of nausea and she picked up her pace a bit, sweat prickling her bare skin.

Only when she finally got home – to the *house* that didn't feel so much like home anymore – did she hear buzzing. She paused at the front door, her heart thumping wildly, and then they landed in perfect unison. Three of them. On the arm she'd raised to slide the key into the lock. A few minutes earlier or later and she might have missed them.

She gasped as they bit as one, three needle stabs as each proboscis pierced her skin and drew a bit of blood, and then they were gone, darting away too quickly for her eyes to follow.

She stared for a long moment at the three minute punctures, three pore-sized drops of blood. Three bites at once. Did that mean something, a sign of some sort, the Holy Trinity perhaps? Better not to read too much into this. More likely so little exposed skin was out and about these days that the sight of it drew a crowd.

She couldn't feel it, of course, but she knew that somewhere within her skin tiny molecules of fly saliva had attached themselves to red blood cells and were even now triggering a reaction. Antibodies would soon flood her bloodstream, attacking her red cells, lysing them and releasing their contents to clog up her already failing kidneys. The lifespan of those dear, oxygen-carrying reds would plunge from three-to-four months to a couple of days.

The reaction wasn't like an infection, taking days and weeks to incubate. In its headlong rush to rid the body of the foreign saliva molecules, the human immune system overreacted and targeted the body's red cells as well, treating them as invaders and beginning to destroy them within hours of the bite. When their number dropped below a critical level, her brain and heart and liver and kidneys would fail from asphyxiation.

At least that was what the "experts" reported. Her nurse training helped her understand what they were saying. They also said the visions of God in the victims' last moments were hallucinations resulting from hypoxia.

Sometimes you had to read the "experts" with a grain of salt. She'd been at the bedside of too many of the dying in their last moments as they saw Him. They couldn't all be having the same hallucination.

No, the visions were real. And now she would enjoy that sacred privilege.

And so it had begun. And right here, on her threshold. God's work. The irony was that years ago God had sent her, unbidden, an autoimmune disorder in the form of lupus. Today she had helped Him give her another.

Somewhere in the distance she heard the spray trucks rumbling along the roads. They belonged to a different world now. She'd expected more fear, now that it was done, but all she felt was calm. A sense of "well, that's that then," as her mother would say when any calamity occurred, from breaking a cooking dish to her diagnosis of terminal cancer. That was that, then. The weight of the lupus was gone too. She doubted it had a chance of killing her now.

She looked to the heavens, said a silent prayer, and then went inside to wait for Nigel. She had to decide whether to tell him of the bites – absolutely not that she'd courted them – or simply let the symptoms begin.

NIGEL

Despite Nigel's call about a murder-suicide, it took the police over an hour to send a single cop around. A young Special Constable named Fitch arrived with lights flashing but no siren and looked squeamish around the bodies. He took statements and said a crime scene team would be out soon.

When Fitch was done, Nigel said, "Were you at all involved in the matter of their missing child?"

Fitch frowned. "Missing child? When did that happen?"

"About ten days ago. You're local?"

He nodded. "Harrow Central. Used to be part time, but with so many out–"

"And no one's ever made mention of Bandora Hakizimana?"

He smiled. "Oh, I believe I'd remember that name, sir. No, no one."

Odd.

Fitch called in again and looked frustrated. "The crime scene investigator is delayed. I'll have to wait until he arrives."

Nigel glanced at Mal who was sitting on the living room sofa gazing off into space as if trying to comprehend what had happened here. He'd known them, after all. Nigel was too wound up to sit.

He went to the front window and stared out at the deserted, sunlit street. Still no sign of the DI.

As he was turning away he spotted a man standing in the shade between two of the houses across the street. He wasn't doing anything, just standing… and looking Nigel's way, as if watching the Hakizimana house.

Nigel leaned closer to the pane, trying to make out his features. He was dark, Indian maybe. His shadowed face… he looked familiar… almost like–

"Wha–?" He jerked back from the window as recognition hit him like a fist to the jaw. "No! It can't–!"

"What's up?" Mal said.

"No fucking way!" Nigel cried, leaping to the door and pulling it open.

He stared through the storm door at the spot between the houses – now empty. He shoved it open and ran across the street through the bright sunlight. He reached the shady spot where the man had stood. Not a trace of him now, but the unmown grass was flattened in a small area. He ran to the rear and scanned the backyards on either side. Empty.

He realized he was out in the open without his ski mask. Christ! Shaking his head, he hurried back to the Hakizimana house.

"Are you daft?" Mal said as he ducked back inside.

"I saw someone watching the house."

"Where?"

Nigel stared through the door at that empty space. "Across the street. I could have sworn–" He stopped himself.

"Sworn what?"

Nigel shook his head. "He looked like Doctor Singh."

"Fuck off!"

"No, I swear." He was shaking inside. "I'm not talking just another Indian guy and they all look alike and that rubbish. I know Singh's face–"

"You've never met him."

"Seen enough photos and it was him!"

Mal sighed. "This was supposed to get your mind off that."

"And it has, but I'm telling you, Mal–"

"Doctor Rajiv Singh is dead. They pulled his body from the embers. You're seeing things, mate."

Was he? Was he really?

He shook his head. "Well, if I am, it's because of this house." He turned and glanced at Constable Fitch. "All right if I step out for some fresh air?"

Fitch nodded. "Just don't wander far. The DI might have a few questions."

"If I wander anywhere it will be to Harrow Central about the boy."

While Fitch had been questioning Mal, Nigel had removed Bandora's sketch from its frame and rolled it into a cylinder. He took this along as he slipped on his gloves and ski mask and stepped out again. He kept watch across the street as he scooted directly next door to another brick house almost identical to the Hakizimanas'. Lifting his mask, he rang the doorbell but stayed outside the screen door. A frumpy, middle-age woman in a shapeless housedress answered. Her eyes were red and teary.

"Yes?" she said, squinting in the light.

"I'm helping the police with an investigation."

"I saw the police car. Is something wrong?"

"There's been an…incident at the Hakizimanas'."

"Who?"

He'd been hoping she'd ask him in but she only stared through the screen. He pointed next door. "The Hakizimanas – your neighbors."

"Oh, the black couple. Never knew their name. Have they got the plague?"

"I'm afraid so."

She sobbed and pulled a tissue from her pocket. "It took my John last week.'

"I'm so sorry."

"He went so fast." She dabbed at her eyes.

"I shouldn't be bothering you."

"No, please. It's good to have somebody to talk to."

Poor woman.

"But you've seen them then? Your neighbors?"

"Now and again. The man, mostly. He gets the mail and opens and closes the garage door, and that's all I see of him. They drive out of the garage and back in later."

Nigel had a feeling this lady was a veteran shade peeper. He unrolled the sketch.

"Does this little boy look familiar?"

She shook her head. "Who is he?"

"The Hakizimanas' child. We're looking for him."

Another shake of her head. "Never knew they had one."

He left her. As he crossed the Hakizimanas' front yard he watched across the street – no sign of anyone. Had he imagined that figure in the shade? He'd seemed so real.

He tried the house on the other side and found an elderly man wearing a portable oxygen concentrator with clear plastic tubing running past his nose. He knew less than the lady.

The DI in charge arrived. He looked tired and irritated; with the aid of their journalist credentials, he accepted the murder-suicide scenario with only a couple of follow-up questions.

He hadn't heard that the Hakizimanas' child was missing either.

"Time for a visit to the station," Nigel said.

Mal nodded. "Bloody right."

BBC:

Of all major industrialized cities, Tokyo appears to be faring the best. Strict pest control measures and quick interment or cremation of the dead have limited the urban impact of the plague. That is not true in the rural regions, however, and that is causing increasing concern. The rural situation, a ticking time bomb, is scheduled for discussion today in the National Diet.

NIGEL

Detective Sergeant Blake looked like he'd lost weight recently. His collar, though buttoned, hung loose around his neck. He knew of the missing boy and pulled the report.

"Came in a little over a week ago," he said.

Nigel tried to read it upside down. "Bandora Hakizimana?"

"If that's how you say it." He shook his head. "Christ, get a human name."

Nigel let that go. "Any progress?"

Blake gave him a bleak look. "You must be joking."

"I assure you he's not," Mal said, letting some anger show. "And neither am I."

Sergeant Blake reddened. "Look, I don't know what planet you're living on, but things around here have changed. We spend the nights chasing looters and the days moving the dead. That's about all we have the time or people for – just had a murder-suicide of a couple of plaguers a couple of hours ago."

"We know," Nigel said. "The boy's parents. We called it in."

"Well, get this: Most of our officers – even DCI's and above – are refusing to work in the daylight hours and are more involved with the looters at night. We're operating half staffed on all shifts and things are getting worse by the hour. So guess what? Any missing person – even your Pandora Hakizaki – is low priority."

"He's just a kid,' Nigel said. 'And now he's an orphan."

Blake sighed. "Well, I'm sorry about that, but we don't have the manpower to go knocking on doors."

"Did they give you a photo at least?" Nigel said.

Blake rechecked the folder. "No. Maybe they said they'd bring one in later."

"Who took the report?" Mal said. "Can we speak to him?"

Blake checked the report again and shook his head. "Crowley. He's gone."

"Where?"

"To the graveyard. Plague."

————

When he and Mal were back in the car, Nigel said, "Do you

think we might have a *Virginia Woolf* situation going on here?"

"What? Some bisexual thing? Bloomsbury? Where are you coming up with this?"

Nigel almost laughed. "No, sorry. I was talking about George and Martha's son in *Who's Afraid of Virginia Woolf.*"

Mal stiffened. "You think Bandora is imaginary?"

"Well, you've never seen him. Has your wife?"

He shook his head. "No."

"The neighbors have never seen him either. There's no photo of him at the house or in the police report. So I've got to ask: Was there ever a child at all?"

Nigel watched Mal chew his upper lip as he mulled that.

Finally he shook his head. "Uwimana was horribly upset that Bandora was missing, too much for just a delusion."

Nigel couldn't help thinking of Abby. "Don't be too sure. Delusions can be stronger than reality. Or at least better."

"Enough to go make out a police report?"

Again, thoughts of Abby. "If you're really into a delusion, you're *into* it. I never saw either of the Hakizimanas before today, but I have a damn strong impression they were heavily into something else."

"What? Drugs? I don't—"

"No. Guilt."

Mal chewed his lip again. "You're right. All the We-do-not-deserve nonsense. Where'd that come from?"

"Sounds like a ton of guilt to me."

"It does. That's what he said when I told him I'd called emergency services."

"That's another thing. Why didn't they call for help when they came down with it? Everyone knows the symptoms now. Why did they stay home, waiting to die?"

Mal shook his head. "Because they didn't 'deserve' help?"

"Not only help. His last line before he blew his brains out: 'We shouldn't see God.' If that's not guilt, then I don't know what is."

"But over what?" Mal looked at him and seemed to read his mind. "Shit."

"Right. The boy. If there really was a boy. How do we find out?"

"Hospitals are no use because Bandora was supposedly two years old, and the Hakizimanas have been here less than that, so he wasn't born here."

Nigel snapped his fingers. "That means, if he exists, they brought him in with them. Immigration!"

Mal was smiling, nodding. "That's it, that's it! We've got contacts in the Immigration Service. I'll get on the phone as soon as we get back."

Nigel leaned back. He felt that curious tingle that told him something was going on… something that might want to avoid the light of day. And nothing he liked more than dragging something like that out into the open.

http://www.youtube.com/watch?v=sg…
EXT: STONEHENGE – DAY

Close on the megaliths. The uprights as well as the lintels are black with flies, crowded so thick and close that no trace of the underlying sarcen stone is visible.

Angle widens to reveal a thin, bearded black man standing bareheaded amid a swarm of flies on the bed of a pickup truck. He is dressed in a traditional maroon agbada embroidered with yellow and green. The loose sleeves fall back as he raises his bony bare arms to Heaven. His hands and fingers are severely gnarled.

MUNGU MAN
(thick Swahili accent)
*I am a Mungu, and I speak to you in the
name of God.*

Angle further widens to reveal about two hundred people crowded close about the truck. They are covered head to foot in protective clothing. In stark contrast to the Mungu man, not a square inch of bare flesh is visible.

MUNGU MAN
(shouting)

I hear people say that flies and plague are
not the work of God, but the work of the devil.
I say to you that it not so. Yes, Beelzebub
was prince of demons and Lord of Flies, but
this is different. These are not ordinary flies.
These are the Flies of the Lord. He created the
Plague to test you and He has created the flies
to bring it to you. The Plague is His judgment,
and you must accept the Lord's judgment.
Do not hide from Him behind your wrappings.
Accept His judgment! Through the Plague He
will choose to draw you to His bosom or send
you forth, as he has done with me and my fellow
Mungu, to speak His truth.

With that, the Mungu man whips the agbada over his head and tosses it aside. He stands naked except for a loincloth. He has smeared his torso and legs with what looks like blood. Whatever it is, the flies dive for it and within seconds he is as coated with flies as the trilithons looming behind him.

A voice cries from within the buzzing mass.

MUNGU MAN
Come! Show you faith! Bare youself to the
Lord's judgment! Accept you fate!

Slowly, in singles and pairs at first, then in ever-growing numbers, the crowd begins to shed its protective layers. They raise their arms and cry out to heaven.

In the background, a massive cloud of flies lifts from the megaliths and swarms toward them. It blackens the air as it descends and engulfs the crowd. And above it all, the Mungu man's voice can be heard crying out to heaven:

MUNGU MAN
Praise be God! Praise be God!

NIGEL

Where most businesses were closed or operating with a skeleton staff, *The Light* was still plugging along, but at half throttle. The humdrum stories of governments and budgets and celebrities who'd got fatter or thinner in recent months had fallen away, overwhelmed by grim news of the domestic and international progress of the plague.

Not that journalists were braver than other people, but as Nigel knew himself, they spent so much time feeling like they were on the outside simply observing, most began to believe that they were immune from the strifes that hit the world. Including the plague.

He unrolled the picture of the missing boy and stared at it as his computer fired up. He preferred it to looking at the monitors around the room, most of which were showing the terrible fire and the mob at the Singhs' house. Was it possible Bandora was still alive? The odds weren't good. Missing children news stories rarely ended well.

"Nigel?"

He looked up to see both Toulson and Mal standing at his desk. Neither was smiling and Toulson's face was tinged with red high in his cheeks – the normal indicator that something had royally pissed him off.

"Your doctor called…" he started.

"The etymologist from the museum," Mal interrupted.

"Yeah, him. Apparently the change in the flies is unlikely to have anything to do with Singh's research. 'Random mutation,' he called it. Fuck knows how he knows, but I guess that's his job." Toulson's voice was low. "He said there were also at least four other research labs working in that area. Two American, one Chinese and one French. Did you know that?"

After a long pause, time almost freezing around him, Nigel shook his head. He couldn't bring himself to speak. The few people close by had stopped working and were all listening into their boss's conversation.

"Jesus Christ, Nigel," Toulson spat the words. "What were you thinking? Why didn't you wait until you had all the information until you brought this to us?"

The words stung, breaking Nigel's moment of shock. "Hang on a minute. You wanted to see me as soon as I got back. And I *didn't* break this. I *was* waiting."

The realization was slowly hitting him. A slow-building tidal wave of nausea. Singh had done nothing wrong, not even accidentally, and now he and his family were all dead. Images filled his head. The desperation of trying to save their daughter regardless of their own safety. The futility of it against the mob filled with anger and hate. That small terrified girl being pushed back into the building.

Malcolm was talking, trying to calm Toulson, but all Nigel could hear was the crackle of flames and the shrieks of a terrified child. Why did he leave that thumb drive behind? Was it the champagne? Had that blurred him? One careless moment. A butterfly's wings in the forest.

"We're going to get roasted for this," Toulson said.

Nigel stared at him, aghast at the man's inept choice of words. Toulson didn't even flinch. Fat. Stupid. Untouchable. That was Toulson. And Nigel had to work for him.

"You're not making sense. *We* didn't break the story."

"But *your* research was used. Fingers are going to be pointing everywhere and—"

"The whole world is fucking falling apart and you're worried about finger pointing?"

"Enough! I don't want you near anything to do with the plague, do you understand? I've just paid your doctor friend twice what you offered him to make sure he stays quiet."

He turned and stormed back to his office, leaving a wake of silence.

"He's lost it," Mal said. "Totally lost it. It wasn't your fault."

Nigel nodded. That wasn't how it felt inside, though, however true it might be. A little girl burned alive because of his information…

He looked down at the picture again. A missing boy. A dead girl. Both too young to be guilty of anything in this fucked-up world. The girl was gone, but Bandora might still be alive. Maybe if Nigel could track him down… if he could put this one thing right then perhaps that would at least balance the scales a bit.

He knew what Abby would say: This was all God's will, all His doing, an opportunity presented from on high.

Nigel sighed and fell back on chaos again. Chaos presupposed an observable system. Where was the system here? Tribal strife in Africa seemed the trigger. If things had been different in Burundi, the Hakizimanas might have stayed there with their son; but even with the strife, they could have emigrated and settled elsewhere, say, the Midlands. Little Bandora still might have gone missing but his disappearance wouldn't have landed on Nigel's doorstep. The little Singh girl would still be dead, yes, but Nigel wouldn't have this chance to balance the scales.

Yet, the chain of events had run from the heart of Africa directly to Nigel's lap. What do you call that? Symmetry? Determinism? Either way it gave him a chill.

The boy's eyes stared dolefully from the sketch.

He wanted a drink. Several.

But no. Later maybe, but not now. He had to stick with this. What the fuck else was there for him to do that was in any way useful? He couldn't save the Singhs, he couldn't save Abby from her religiosity. Maybe this was his lifeline. Something to keep him sane in the swarm of madness swallowing up the world.

Nigel began his usual round of searches on the couple – analyzing the Hakizimanas' lives from the paper trails left in their wake. By the time he'd escaped the office for a coffee and a call to Abby – no answer – and returned slightly calmer than when he'd left, his inbox had a few morsels waiting for him.

Raw data could tell you a lot about a person. The Hakizimanas had very few debts, and the two credit cards they used were always paid off, if not in their entirety each month, then pretty damn close. They did not live beyond their means, and if they had fictionalized their child then they were both sharing the delusion. Their shopping habits – mainly done online – showed up the usual items of toys and children's books and toddler pull-ups bought at regular intervals.

He moved on, picking at the Internet and what it could give him. He typed in various spellings of "Zahran", the word they'd cried out in their dying moments, before one led to a YouTube video of a crazy Mungu dressed as some kind of priest being consumed by flies and calling on his worshippers to do the same. Was that Zahran?

Great. More religion. Just what he needed. Was that Stonehenge? He was pretty sure it was. He watched the video again, fascinated by its macabre nature. It somehow reminded him of those old cult horror films like *The Wicker Man*. Was this some kind of Voodoo? Probably. The black man's accent was thick; African not Arab, and his eyes were wild as he scanned the crowd. Plenty of people were buying into his madness, but Nigel couldn't make out the Hakizimanas among them. At the end, a young man at the front dived in front of the camera, his face full of excited religious zeal, and shouted "On to Glastonbury! Glastonbury next!" and then the film ended.

Nigel noted down the date the video was uploaded and then searched the name again, but found nothing of any use. Whoever this Zahran guy was, his followers weren't tweeting or blogging about him. Not that it mattered. He was gone now. Had to be. Mungu or not, no one could survive that many fly bites and not get the plague.

His inbox pinged again, and he closed down the search. The electoral register and council tax info was in. Both had the couple and Bandora listed as living in the Harrow home – so much for the idea of a George-and-Martha delusion – but along with someone else. Another Hakizimana. Jengo. Male.

His skin tingled as his journalistic hackles rose. Here was something. The man, about ten years younger than the couple, had lived with them for several months and then moved out five months previously.

Nigel dialed through to Mal's desk.

"Yep."

Mal sounded tired, and Nigel didn't blame him.

"Did you ever meet a Jengo Hakizimana? I think he must have been Gahiji's brother."

"No. The name's new to me. Why?"

"He stayed with them for a while. I'm going to track him down. See what he knows."

"Great. Thanks. I think I'm going to be chained to my desk for a while managing both Toulson and this shit. I'm not sure I'll be much help for a few days."

"That's okay." Nigel was already tapping Jengo's details into an email. "You know I'm better working on my own. And anyway, if I can trust anyone to cover my arse here, then it's you. Toulson'll hang me out to dry if it comes down to needing a scapegoat. The bastard will probably enjoy it too."

HENRY

After knocking half a dozen times on the door to Alex's flat, Jamie tried the knob. It turned and the door pushed in a bit.

"Uh-oh. That's not good." He glanced at Henry. "Alex's got half a dozen locks on the inside."

His brother's old mate hadn't shown up at the pub today – not that much was left to drink there anyway – and hadn't been answering his phone. Jamie had been worried about him so he'd dragged Henry over to his flat to check up. Henry hadn't wanted to come. He feared going out in public, but Jamie had insisted.

They'd switched their bee hats for ski masks. The bee hat had hidden his face from the TV cameras in Camden or else he'd have been nicked by now for sure. Since Camden anyone with a bee hat was under suspicion, so they'd left theirs home.

With a worried look at Henry, Jamie said, "Here goes," and pushed the door.

It swung open to reveal Alex lying in a recliner under a tattered blanket in the front room. He looked a mess, all pale and exhausted. His unwashed gray hair had gone stringy and bits of food – was that fried rice? – dotted his beard. He held a carving knife in his hand.

"Oh, it's you," he said with a relieved expression.

A laptop sat on the blanket. Arrayed around him on the wall were posters from *The X Files* ("The Truth Is Out There"), *Close Encounters*, *Red Dawn*, and *Enemy of the State*.

His expression hardened as he spotted Henry. "You're all right, Jamie, but here, what're you thinking, bringing that bloody maniac 'round to my place?"

Henry couldn't meet Alex's angry stare. He hadn't been able to make eye contact with anyone except Jamie since Camden. Had it only been yesterday? Jamie understood – well, said he did. A little. Henry had no clear memory of the incident, but he'd seen the horrific YouTube video and recognized himself. How could he have committed such an atrocity? What had he been thinking?

Well, no, he hadn't been thinking – that was the problem. He remembered a red rage, a blinding rush toward vengeance, but he didn't remember lifting that child and tossing her back through the window into the flames. It seemed unimaginable now.

"We ain't heard from you," Jamie said. "And you ain't been answering your phone."

"I been feeling sick," Alex said.

"You could still answer your phone."

"No, I can't." Another hard glare at Henry. "Someone tracked me down. Saw me with that monster there on the video and been ringing me up."

"They saw your face because you were only wearing that little surgical thing,' Jamie said. "And that's why you're sick, innit. You been running around all this time without protection and got yourself bit by a fly."

"Weren't no fly and this ain't no plague. Just feeling a bit rough, that's all.' He pointed to a couple of bottles on the table beside the chair. 'I got the preventology for the plague right here. Megadoses of C and E.'

Henry repressed a disgusted head shake. This twat believed the weirdest loads of cobblers. And he had the plague, sure as shit. This was the way Henry's Maggie and Livvy had started with it.

"Where'd you hear that rubbish?" Jamie said, echoing his thoughts.

Alex patted his laptop. "Internet. Gotta know the right sites to get the straight dope." He put the computer aside and held out a hand. "Here, mate. Help me up then. I gotta hit the loo."

As Jamie pulled Alex out of the chair and helped him down the hall, Henry glanced at the laptop screen and wondered what the dying man – not that he'd admit it – was watching. He leaned over and saw a YouTube video. He started to jerk back, afraid it was the one from last night in Camden, but no, this was different. This had Stonehenge in the background and was freeze-framed on a man up front...

A man covered in flies.

Fascinated, Henry tapped the touchpad and the scene came to life. Some African telling everyone to go out and let the flies bite you. Well, that was pure bollocks, but that man... with his coat of flies... Henry couldn't look away. An idea began to form.

No, more than an idea. A plan. It exploded in his head like a supernova. He knew exactly what he had to do.

NIGEL

It didn't take long to get what he needed. Everyone was trying to claim something these days and Jengo Hakizimana was no different. His income support and housing benefit were registered to a flat on a grotty estate a few miles from where his brother's family had lived and by late afternoon Nigel was standing outside it.

The lift was covered in graffiti and stank of urine and so Nigel took the stairs. By the time he reached the fourth floor he was drenched in sweat under his heavy layers. The corridors and stairwells were eerily empty of bored kids looking for someone to harass and the contained heat had made them unbearably humid. He pulled off his ski mask and breathed with the relief of it. They were all living in fear, and that had unified the nation somewhat, but as he knocked on the door, Nigel was glad that he was living in fear under better circumstances.

No one answered, and he knocked again, louder this time. Inside, music throbbed loud and low with a heavy street R & B sound. Finally someone fiddled with locks and latches on the other side. A heat wave escaped the darkened doorway, carrying a heady mix of sweat and ganja smoke as a thin girl of about twenty-five frowned at him.

"Yeah?" the girl said. "Did Freddie send you? Have you got the stuff?"

Her blond hair was pulled back in an untidy pony tail and her joggers sat on her hipbones. Her vest T-shirt stopped at her belly button, leaving a few inches of skin bare. Nigel suddenly felt very over-dressed.

"I'm looking for Jengo. Is he here?"

"Freddie didn't send you?"

"Sorry, no. It's about his family. It's important."

"He's not here."

"Is it Freddie?" A male shout came from somewhere behind her. Slurred. Lethargic.

"Look, can I come in?" he said.

The girl frowned again. In her stoned state she was clearly having a problem computing that he wasn't Freddie, whoever the fuck that was.

"Okay," she nodded, relieved to have made a decision.

She stepped aside to give him room before closing the door behind him, sealing them in the gloom. All the curtains and blinds were closed and Nigel didn't mind. From what he could make out it wasn't as if anyone was taking too much care of the place. He followed her into a room that could have been a bedroom or lounge originally, but now had a small portable TV in the corner and two mattresses on the floor against each wall. The floor was littered with cans and drug paraphernalia, torn up cigarette packets, Rizlas and lighters and, to the side of one of the makeshift bed/sofas, a couple of small crack pipes, their bowls darkly stained.

Two men in jeans and sweatshirts sat cross-legged on one mattress and one was skinning up. At least they weren't on the crack. He'd never get any information out of them.

"He's looking for Jeng," the girl said, dropping to the other mattress.

Nigel didn't sit down. The flies outside were bad, but fuck only knew what was living in those stained beds. He stood with his back to a grimy window and faced them in the dying light.

"He's not here," one of the men said.

He lit the spliff and drew in heavily. Food supplies were dwindling but drugs were still plentiful. Amazing. Nigel sensed no menace in the room. They might be druggies, but they weren't dealers.

"Yeah, I get that," Nigel said. "I need to speak to him. His family... his brother... he's dead. A kid's missing."

"Shit, man."

"Everyone's dying," added the other youth, a white kid with a bad case of acne, and shook his head wearily as if he'd said something truly profound.

"Do you know where he is?" Nigel asked.

He focused on the black man with the joint. He seemed the straightest. Not that there was much in it.

"Been gone a week." He looked over at the girl. "That's about right, isn't it?"

"Yeah," she nodded. "I think. Maybe a little longer. After his last giro got paid."

Just over a week. Ten days? That was when the boy vanished. Could Jengo have taken him? Maybe that was why the parents felt so guilty as they were dying. They'd trusted their child to someone and they were wrong.

Nigel tried to keep his tone light. "Do you know where he went?"

She sniggered at the question and leaned over and took the joint.

"What's funny?"

"He tripped out, didn't he, Sam. Kept saying he had something that was going to save us all."

"He lost it," said Sam, the black man. "Cloud crazy. Talking about 'mungu' and 'old ways' and shit like that. Don't know where he went."

The white kid said, "Didn't he mention Glastonbury or something?"

The girl sniggered again. "Glastonbury? As if. There's no Glasto this year."

"Told us he'd be back though," Sam said. "To save us." His turn to laugh.

"Did he say what he'd found?"

Sam shrugged. "Didn't really listen. He was out a lot. Just talked mad shit."

Nigel thought back to the YouTube video and the dying couple's last words.

"Did he mention a Zahran ever? That word mean anything to you?"

"No, man, sorry," Sam said.

The white kid came out of his haze. "Yeah, he did. Yeah, I heard him say that. He was chanting some shit. That word was in it."

"Religious chanting?"

The kid looked at him like he was stupid. "What other kind of chanting is there?"

He had a point.

"Anybody got a picture of him?"

"As if," the girl said again. "Hey wait."

She pulled out her phone – an older iPhone – and did a lot of thumbing. Finally...

"There." She handed it to Nigel. "Group portrait."

He saw four people grouped around a bong, grinning. Three of them were right here in the room. The fourth had a very black face and a very blond afro.

"That's him with the bleached hair?"

"Yeah," said Sam. "Tries to tell you that's the real color but we know he bleaches it."

Nigel handed back the phone. As they skinned up some more and carried on waiting for the mythical Freddie, he gave them twenty quid, throwing it down on the floor rather than touching any of them.

As he turned to make his exit he glanced out the window and saw someone who could only be Rajiv Singh staring up at him from the shadowed pavement across the street, four stories below.

He bolted for the door and raced down the stairs, almost tripping twice in his haste. When he reached the street the man was gone.

He stood there panting, eyes closed. Was he losing it? He didn't believe in ghosts, so was he totally hallucinating, or simply putting Singh's face on other people? He hadn't been masked or gloved like everyone else. Had to be a hallucination.

He shook it off. Forget Singh – no, never forget him, but put him aside for now and center on that little boy. He focused on the kernel of excitement in his stomach.

Too many links for coincidence. Jengo had left his doper friends around the time the boy went missing and he had a thing for this Zahran character. Maybe Jengo was in some drug psychosis that made him think the boy was a kind of messiah. Someone who could save them all? No great leap from Abby's own resolute fatalism. Could Jengo have taken the boy and gone looking for Zahran?

Suddenly Nigel felt the drive of energy that came with seeing the pieces start to fall together. He was going to find that boy. And save him from his crazy uncle.

ABBY

The afternoon had passed slowly as Abby waited for Nigel to come home, a small knot of anxiety growing in the pit of her stomach. Not of fear for herself – she was quite at peace with whatever fate God chose for her – but because she knew that whatever problems they'd had recently, beneath it all, Nigel still loved her. This would hurt him terribly, and she hated that.

Outside, the day grew heavier and more humid, as if the spirit of the coming storm was seeping through the clouds and into the air close to the ground and the pressure was too oppressive to do anything more than just sit. For a while she'd watched the TV. Live shows were few and far between – too many on-screen talent and off-screen crew sick, she imagined. They re-ran old sitcoms instead, but she couldn't focus and in the end turned it off, preferring the quiet peace.

She's thought about having a glass of wine but in the end sat and drank hot tea in the kitchen and listened to the clock ticking the minutes away as the sky became a darker gray. The storm would come tonight, as inevitable as a fight with Nigel, and she wanted both to be over.

Three days. She could feel the steady thump of her heart pulsing gently through her. Strange to think three days might be all she had left. Two really. By the third most victims weren't entirely conscious. Not until the end anyway. She shivered slightly with a tingle of excitement. Not until they saw the light. God. Him.

Was it wrong that she was looking forward to it? She felt like a sheep that had been lost on a mountainside in freezing winter and had finally found its way back to the flock. She wondered when she'd notice the symptoms, and felt the first flutter of nerves. Not because she was sure death was coming to find her, but because she hoped it wouldn't be too painful. She'd heard that the plague was relatively kind to its victims. She'd find out soon enough. Hearsay was becoming her reality. *The* plague was now *her* plague.

"Abby?"

She jumped slightly as the front door closed and Nigel's footfalls came fast along the corridor.

"Abby? Where are you?"

"In here."

"Two ticks, I'm desperate for the loo."

He sounded different. The resigned tone that he normally tried hard to disguise when he got home was gone. After the tragedy of the Singhs she'd expected him to be in black mood. What had happened?

She got up and pulled two wine glasses down from the cupboard. Sod the tea. This was going to take something stronger.

She'd decided to tell him about the bites. But how? She'd just have to blurt it out. She needed to tell him during whatever good mood he was in. She wanted him to stay with her while she died. Not for her own comfort, although it would also bring that, but because perhaps if he saw her interaction with God then he would finally realize that all this is His work. Part of His plan. Maybe her role in all this was to bring Nigel into the light? Not such a crazy thought. If ever a man needed saving, if only from himself, Nigel was it. He'd always railed so hard against the world. Perhaps it was time he had some peace.

The toilet flushed and few moments later he joined her, taking the glass.

"We need to talk," he said.

Oh boy, do we.

"There's this kid," he carried on after a long sip of wine. "He's gone missing. Only two years old. Part of Mal's extended family. His parents died this morning, but I think he's been taken by a relative. I think I can find him. It's a long shot I know, but after everything that's happened – the Singhs, their little girl – I just think maybe, maybe this is one good thing I can do. Something real. Something that actually matters."

His words were coming out in a rush and she found their content mattered less than the energy behind them. She hadn't seen Nigel this motivated – this *alive* – in a long time. She might not be the old Abby but he sounded like the old Nigel.

"You know where they've gone?" she asked. Her fly bites itched, urging her to release the truth.

"The southwest I think. Glastonbury. There's some cult moving around. Going there next I think. I need to do some more digging into the man who's taken him, but I'm pretty sure that's where he's gone."

"You're going after him?" she asked, sipping her own wine. Her mouth was dry.

"I'd like to." For the first time his voice lost some of its power. "But frankly I'm afraid to leave you after…"

The sentence drained away and she saw the conflict in his face. He didn't want to argue any more than she did. Suddenly, the truth of the situation struck her, and as it did, rain began to fall in thick drops outside, tapping against the window.

"Oh, don't worry about that," she said, keeping her eyes on his as she lied. "Been there, didn't do that. Won't even think of doing that again. Really, I'm sorry. It was a stupid thought."

"You're sure?" he asked, his eyes narrowing suspiciously.

"Very sure."

That wasn't a lie. It was suddenly becoming clear to her that her path and Nigel's were not the same. If she told him now that she'd been bitten, he wouldn't leave. And then who would go after the boy? Surely, saving one innocent life in the midst of all this was a mission from God Himself, even if Nigel didn't realize it yet. She needed to let him go. He needed to find his own way into the light. She was surprised at how much that hurt her heart. The idea of him leaving and never seeing him again.

Not in this world at any rate.

"You think this child is in danger?" she said.

"We're all in danger, but yes." He looked at her. "It probably sounds crazy, but I can't help but think that if I can find him, get him back to Mal and his family, then maybe, just maybe, something will be right in the world."

"Then you should do it." She smiled, softly. "You have to." He watched her thoughtfully and she forced her smile into a grin. "I'll be on the other end of the phone line. We get on better that way, anyway."

He looked at her. "Are you sure?"

His mind was made up, she could see that, and she needed to release him from his guilt.

"Absolutely." She meant it. "This is a good thing you're doing. And if anyone can find him, you can. I trust you."

"I love you, Abby," he said, after a moment, and then stood up and pulled her close.

Such a long time since he'd done that so willingly and she could have burst into tears against his chest.

"I love you too, Nigel." She drank in his scent and then pushed him away gently. "You'd better go and pack then. If you're going to be traveling then you'll be safer at night." She glanced out at the darkening sky. "Especially in a storm."

He was already on his phone, to Mal probably, and heading up the stairs by the time she'd finished her glass of wine. She'd go to church when he'd gone. Help those who were afraid. Pray for Nigel. Pray for all of them on their solitary paths. She just hoped that his would lead him to the light. That they could be there together.

NO PLAGUE IN NORTH KOREA
(For Immediate Release)
PYONGYANG - the Health Ministry of the Democratic People's Republic of Korea has announced to the world that North Korea has yet to experience a single case of the mysterious plague infecting the capitalist world. This is attributed to the superior vermin control practiced by the citizens of North Korea under the guidance of their

illustrious leader, Kim Jong-Un, who has forbidden
infected flies from crossing into North Korean airspace.
Due to his lustrous influence, the workers' paradise that
is the Democratic People's Republic of Korea remains
gloriously free of the plague.

ABBY

Nigel closed the front door just as the first flash of lightning cracked the sky outside. She went upstairs and watched him from the bedroom window, leaving the lights off so he wouldn't glance up and have second thoughts about going. His head was down against the rain as he jogged across the street and the indicators flashed on the Audi before he'd even reached the pavement. Within thirty seconds he was out of view behind the wheel and gone. That was that.

Abby didn't move. She waited to feel something. Not the sudden emptiness of the house around her. She'd expected that now that her husband had left and their home was likely to become her tomb. She waited to feel something shift inside her from well to unwell.

She pulled up a chair and sat by the window. Something mesmerizing about watching the storm crashing across the city and the heavy sheets of water pounding the empty pavements below. Most likely this would be the last storm she ever saw. In the houses opposite she could just make out a tiny glow of yellow here and there escaping from the tiniest cracks in the curtains and shutters and netting. Many people had all three. It made her half-smile. Flies weren't that easy to keep out. Just like their God.

Her mind drifted until, an hour or so later, the storm finally moved on, its rage quieting until all she could hear was the occasional echo of thunder in the distance. Water hung in ragged drops from every surface outside. Abby stretched in the chair and got to her feet. She still felt perfectly fine and now she was restless. She pushed open the window. Even after the rain the air was still hot and sticky and she stretched one arm out like a child to feel it. It felt good.

She grabbed her keys but didn't take her wallet. Nothing would be open this late, and hardly anything was left to buy anyway. She'd started a subconscious clock after the bites and it was ticking backward from seventy-two. By the time it hit twelve she'd probably be all but unconscious. After church she'd go to the hospital and do what she could to comfort the dying… before she joined them and the Lord claimed her. She missed Dr. Kumaran – they said he'd come down with the plague – but that meant they needed her more than ever.

NIGEL

The drive out of London was a sobering one. The streets should have been clogged with Saturday night traffic, and the downpour should have royally snarled it. But he cruised unimpeded through the rain.

The city itself had gone into shutdown, and though the news on the radio declared that everything was under control, clearly it was not. The flies were in control.

He wondered how it could have reached this point so quickly. How many others had come through the airports like the man he'd seen at Heathrow. Some would be religious nutters and others would just be bitter people who didn't want to go out alone. Humanity was its own worst enemy – to believe that a caring God was at work in all this was madness of the highest order. At least if Abby stayed inside, she'd be relatively protected.

As he hit the motorway, the storm waned but the overhead lights hadn't come on, leaving only the rare set of headlights coming the other way to brighten the journey. He turned off the radio and zoned out in the silence, letting time tick by as he drifted between memories of *before* and *now* and how much the world had changed. He found he wondered what would be *after*, and whether he'd even be a part of it.

Sheep dotted the fields like clouds on a dusky sky, and in the growing gloom cows called to each other, the sound an ache. Unmilked, Nigel thought. Unmilked and unaware.

He tried the radio again and found some terrible 80s compilation of hits, including REM's "It's the End of the World." Trouble was, he didn't feel fine.

He was glad when he finally pulled into the drive of Meare

Manor. He'd done an Internet search before leaving and had settled on this two-story stone hotel as his base of operations. Situated on the moors a mile or two northwest of town, the small estate had once served as the summer retreat for the monks at Glastonbury Abbey.

Night now having fallen, he parked as close to the entrance as possible and pulled on his ski mask and gloves before grabbing his bag and laptop to run inside, closing the door firmly behind him. Checking in didn't take long. He was the only guest they had, and the woman who explained breakfast and dinner – apparently food was still in decent supply out here in the country – and got him a glass of wine to take to his room, was almost desperately happy to see him; as if having a guest was a return to normalcy.

Nigel was happy to close his bedroom door behind him and have some peace. His room was spacious, with a king bed and a little sitting area and a couple of easy chairs. A flat-screen TV hung on the wall. At another time he might have appreciated it all, but the world was turning too crazy too fast, and all he wanted was a shower and a good sleep before focusing on his search for Bandora.

SUNDAY

NIGEL

He slept far later than he'd meant to. A quick phone call to reception and breakfast came on a tray to his room, courtesy of a teenage boy – probably the owner's son. When he was finished and showered he headed out with Bandora's picture to ask the locals if they'd seen the boy. It was nearly midday and the summer warmth was stifling in all his protective clothing.

The tor loomed over the village, its green curves bright in the sunlight, and at its peak he could see the tower, all that remained of an ancient church. He'd half-expected to see Zahran and his followers gathered there, given the place's reputation as a holy and spiritual site, but nothing but empty nature gazed down on him. He focused on his search. Looking for the boy was all he had, and he was determined to find him.

Three hours later and his determination was eaten up by his frustration.

"Total fucking waste of time," he muttered, pulling his gloves off with his teeth before starting the car again.

After fruitless attempts to show Bandora's sketch to the few locals he could find, he'd called it a day. Most weren't answering their doors, and the local pub was closed. Those he'd managed to pin down for a few minutes were eager to get rid of him and barely glanced at the picture. A lot of people had passed through, they said. But no, they hadn't seen him, or a young black man with bleached hair. The place was a virtual ghost town. Without tourists coming through and with no music festival, businesses had closed. Whereas it might have been home to eight or nine thousand folks a few months ago, now he'd be surprised if the locals numbered a thousand, and *nothing* was happening.

Then again, maybe Bandora wasn't here at all. But that didn't mean he wouldn't be. The video had said Zahran was coming to Glastonbury but it hadn't said when. Maybe they hadn't arrived yet.

Still, he pounded his frustration against the steering wheel as he turned into the driveway along the side of Meare Manor. He wanted to find the boy and get back to Abby in London.

He parked around the back and entered through the rear. On his way to the stairs he glanced in the dining room where afternoon tea was being served to a solitary man, a new arrival at the hotel perhaps. Nigel stopped cold. The man, sitting with his back to him, had slightly wavy black hair and a dusky complexion. God damn, if it wasn't the Indian who'd been dogging him. Well, he wasn't getting away this time.

Nigel strode up behind him and grabbed his shoulder.

"What the hell are you–?"

The startled face that looked up at him was Indian, all right, but had a thick mustache and bore not the slightest resemblance to Rajiv Singh.

"I beg your pardon?" he said, blinking nervously.

"Oh, Christ." Embarrassed, Nigel raised his hands and backed away. "Sorry-sorry. Thought you were someone else. My bad."

Shaking his head, he found the stairs and trotted up to the second floor. He dropped into one of the easy chairs and pulled out his phone. Abby answered on the second ring.

"'Lo?"

"You sound tired."

"Dialysis always tires me out. You know that."

He did. She'd been doing five hours up to five days a week, and it always left her knackered.

"How's it going there?" she added.

"Miserable."

He vented some of his frustration while she made sympathetic noises, then he turned it back to her – or rather, them. They did get along better when apart, and absence did indeed make his heart grow fonder. Last night, alone here in that big bed, he realized he hadn't truly appreciated how much she meant to him until he'd been faced with the prospect of her death.

"I'm so glad you're taking care of yourself, Abby. You... you mean the world to me."

He didn't know how he'd expected her to respond, but he hadn't expected a sob.

"Are you all right?"

"Yes," she said with a shaky voice.

"Then–?"

"Please don't be nice to me."

Baffled, he said, "I don't understand."

Her little laugh sounded forced. *"Oh, ignore me. It's that time of the month and along with the dialysis my head's all over the place. I just need a good night's sleep."*

After a little more small talk Nigel let her go. She did sound tired. He hoped that was all it was. Worry niggled at him. Something in her voice... How bad had London got overnight?

He turned on the TV for distraction and was shocked to find half the stations off the air. There was his answer. He hadn't tuned in since before leaving for Africa. Everything really was falling apart, wasn't it. And here he was in deserted, godforsaken Glastonbury searching for a kid who probably was somewhere back in London.

"Fuck it!"

He turned off the TV and fired up his laptop. At least the Internet was still working. He did what he did every time he sat down at a computer of late: hit Google and searched for Zahran. And every time he was rewarded with the same old links, all colored mauve because he'd already clicked on them.

No, wait. Here was a blue one – a YouTube video posted just today – less than an hour ago. It took his anxious index finger three tries on the touchpad before the arrow landed on the link. He clicked and a few seconds later a wizened figure appeared on the screen. Nigel knew that wild salt-and-pepper hair and even grayer beard from repeated viewings of the first video. Same voice, same Swahili accent, even the same words as he raised his arms.

I am a Mungu, and I speak to you in the name of God...

Nigel had a momentary sinking feeling as he realized Zahran was wearing the same maroon-yellow-green agbada as before and standing on the same pickup truck. Was this the old Stonehenge appearance shot from a different angle? But no... no megaliths behind him this time. Some other sort of stone ruins—

"Christ!"

He jumped up and headed for the door. They weren't going to the Tor, at all. That had been shot in the ruins of Glastonbury Abbey – not three miles from here.

ABBY

She hadn't been sure she'd know when the plague symptoms hit. She didn't see much point in doing dialysis if the plague was going to carry her off, so she'd already been feeling crummy. Her fatigue and general malaise weren't from the plague; it took a while for it to drop the blood count significantly. Besides, despite the marrow booster injections she'd been getting, she was already anemic from the kidney failure.

But the plague wasn't sneaky. The aches came during the night, and when they hit – with flulike severity – she knew she was on her way.

She'd read enough articles in the papers and online, and talked to enough victims about the early signs. The widespread muscle aches were due to the rupturing red cells releasing all their hemoglobin into her bloodstream. Strange to think of all those tiny explosions going off inside her. Her body was a universe in itself, and soon she would leave its mysteries behind and become part of a more glorious existence. A new life, in the light of the Lord. If only she didn't have to leave Nigel behind. But then, given the way the world was crumbling around them, their separation was bound to be short-lived.

She'd hated lying to him about the dialysis, about her period, but what choice did she have? If she told him she had the plague he'd abandon his search and rush back to be at her side. He needed to find that boy. Maybe if he could feel redeemed in his own eyes, he could find redemption in the Lord when the inevitable time came.

Still, her joy at becoming closer to God was dampened by all the things she wanted to tell Nigel, her husband in the eyes of God and the love of her life, but would never get to say.

Wait…Nigel's camera took videos. She could record herself; she could say all the things she wanted him to hear, explain why she'd chosen this path. She could say good-bye and…

Yes. A fizz of energy ran through her tired bones. She had to find the camera and get this done while she still had the strength. Tomorrow might be too late.

NIGEL

What's Zahran doing? Nigel thought as he drove through the center of town. Touring the country's religious sites? In some respect that made sense. If he considered himself the savior of mankind then it would be natural to go to places believed to possess spiritual worth. Perhaps as the news of his journey spread, more desperate followers would show up in the hope of escaping death.

Nigel hoped he was still there. He hadn't checked the abbey grounds earlier, figuring if the town was damn near deserted, the ruins would be even less populated.

As the only car on the road, he made excellent time following the signs to Abbey Park. He found the parking lot – no shortage of spaces – and adjusted his ski mask before stepping into the twilight. He spotted some of the ruins above the trees and so he headed that way.

He'd expected to find Abbey Park as deserted as the rest of the town but when he came round a thick oak trunk he found a sort of canvas city instead. He stopped and surveyed the motley assortment of tents and even a few RVs. It was like the ghost of Glastonbury festival – but with bands like the Grateful Dead or Phish – except no music filled the air and no one looked too happy.

A man in camo fatigues stood outside a pup tent sucking on a joint though the mouth hole of a black balaclava, filling the air between them with the smell of tobacco mixed with the sweet herb.

"Is Zahran still here?" Nigel pulled out the picture of the boy. He had no time for dicking around. "I think he might be able to help me find this kid."

The guy stared at him. "It's you."

"What's me? This boy's name is Bandora. He's missing."

"No, I mean, they been lookin' for you." The man turned and hurried off to the right. "Oi, Rachard! Boynt! That bloke you're lookin' for – 'e's 'ere!"

Looking for me? Nigel thought with a pang of uneasiness. No one knew he was in Glastonbury except Abby – not even Mal. And even if someone did know, why would they be looking for him?

Oh, the sketch, of course. Word must have gotten back about him. But why would the sketch interest them that much? Unless...

The stoner returned with a skinny black guy sporting thick dreads and a beefy white baldy, neither wearing shirt nor mask.

"Walked right up to me and asked me about the Mungu, 'e did. Showed me the picture, as well."

"Yeah, it's him all right," said the black with a faint Jamaican accent. "Or at least he's wearing the same mask. You been showin' pictures of a kid around?"

Nigel sensed a certain amount of tension coiling around the two. Why? He was hardly the intimidating sort.

"Well, not pic*tures*, exactly," Nigel said, emphasizing the plural. "But this sketch–"

"You're the one then," the black said, grabbing his arm. "Right. You're coming with us."

Nigel pulled back. "Whoa. Coming where?"

"Didn't you want to see the Mungu?"

"I wanted to see Zahran."

"Same difference. He wants to see you too."

"Good. We're all on the same page then." He pulled his arm free. "But I'll walk on my own, thank you very much."

"Fair enough." He nodded toward the white guy. "But you've got to let Boynt here pat you down."

"Why? I'm not here to hurt anyone."

"I'm sure you aren't, brother. But the plague's made a lotta people crazy out there. We gotta be careful."

Nigel raised his arms and Boynt did a quick but efficient pat down.

A former copper maybe?

"Let's go," the black guy said, leading the way.

"I'm Nigel." He figured giving them his name wouldn't hurt. He glanced over his shoulder. "Boynt?"

"Boynton."

"First name?"

"Last."

Talkative sort.

"And so you must be Rachard. Interesting name."

"If you say so, mon."

He didn't look back and Nigel moved a little closer to him as they wound their way among the ramshackle arrangement of tents and trailers and RVs. Here and there large candles on sticks burned and several fires blazed in old drums, sending shadows and light across the makeshift community. "How long've you been camped here?"

"A while."

Details were going to be hard to get out of his companions it seemed.

"I saw a video of your Mungu at Stonehenge–"

"That was a while back. Hardly anyone who was there is left."

"The plague?"

He nodded without turning. "Some. And some crazy pagans turned up claiming Stonehenge was theirs. But the plague got most, yeah. But that's all changed now that we've got the Cure."

The dopers had mentioned Jengo talking about a cure. Not that Nigel believed it for a minute, but he decided to play along.

"A cure? Really? Shouldn't you be sharing it with the world?"

Rachard was shaking his head as Boynt spoke from behind. "Ain't enough to go 'round."

"Believers only, mon," Rachard added. "Believers only."

They stopped before a larger tent that sat in the shadow of what once might have been the entrance to the abbey and where two burly men in combats stood either side of the flap, neither disguising the handguns tucked into their belts. If the boy was inside, Nigel wasn't going to be able to grab him and run. One of them held up a tent flap and Rachard said something through it before nodding back at Nigel.

"You can see him."

Nigel stepped into the tent – and fought to keep from recoiling at the stench. Sweat – yeah, he'd expected that with no showers available – but something else too… something rotten. A quick scan of the interior showed a kerosene lantern, a small table, a couple of suitcases, and a bedroll. Nowhere to hide a little boy. The man himself was sitting cross-legged beside the table, looking exactly like he did in the videos, although close up in the grimy light, the lines on his face made him look a thousand years old, leathery and mummified.

"Sit. Take off you mask,' he said in that thick accent. "Zahran wish to see you face."

Well, the sun was down and the flies were grounded, so why not? He tugged it off. The air felt good on his skin. He lowered himself to the ground and mimicked Zahran's pose.

Zahran stared at him a moment, then frowned. "I am told man is looking for little African boy. This man is you?'

Nigel nodded.

"You are police?"

"No."

Zahran smiled, revealing surprisingly white teeth, and Nigel couldn't help but feel he'd stepped into some surreal movie where he was facing an Indian chief.

"Why does white Englishman look for African boy?"

"Long story, I'm afraid."

"Tell me. We have time."

Nigel took a breath and sighed. "His name's Bandora Hakizimana and he was living in London with his parents when his uncle, a kid called Jengo, took off with him about ten days ago."

Nigel didn't mention that he only *assumed* Jengo had taken off with him.

"You an investigator?" Boynt said. The two goons had followed him inside but stayed close to the entrance. "Private like? His folks hire you?"

Nigel wondered if Boynt had just used up all his words for the night. He also wondered how much he should tell them. Oh, hell, go for it.

"I'm a journalist and his parents died of the plague."

"He is orphan." Zahran said. He didn't sound surprised. Then, why should he?

"Yes."

"You are friends of his parents?"

"No. I met them only once. Briefly."

Very briefly.

"You know this boy, then?"

Nigel shook his head. "Never met him. Never laid eyes on him."

"Then how can you find him?"

Nigel pulled the sketch from his pocket and handed it to Zahran. The Mungu's gnarled fingers unfolded the sheet and studied it.

"This is all you have? No photograph?"

"That's all."

"Is there a reward?" Rachard said.

Nigel shook his head again. "Not a penny."

Zahran's frown deepened. "I do not understand. Again, I ask why white Englishman looks for little African boy? In the midst of all…" he gestured delicately with one hand. "This."

Dare he say, *redemption*? No.

"His parents were friends of a friend. He was taken without permission. We're both concerned about his safety."

Zahran's eyes bore into his. "You are an interesting man."

"Can you help me? Have you seen Bandora?"

"Perhaps he has found me."

His dark eyes were unreadable, but Nigel felt a surge of triumph. It wasn't a no. Here was the break he'd been looking for.

"Where is he? Can I see him? The kid, Jengo, had bleached hair. Maybe you remember him?"

"You will find boy when you are ready."

Shit. He had no time for this mumbo-jumbo bullshit.

"I'm ready now. Like you say, there's a lot of crap going on and I want to get him back to London."

"The boy will find you when he is ready. Everything is a test of faith."

"I'm not really the believing kind." Nigel tried to keep the irritation out of his voice. Clearly Zahran knew something otherwise why the fuss of bringing him here. But what?

Zahran shrugged. "Perhaps not yet. But you are a good man I feel." He looked at Nigel for a few long seconds and then sniffed as if a decision had been made. "I have something for you."

At last. Maybe some useful information.

Zahran reached beneath the table and produced a mortar and pestle. The bowl – Nigel had never been able to keep straight which was the mortar and which the pestle – was half filled with a granular beige powder. Maybe this was the reason Zahran spoke in riddles. Maybe he was off his face on something.

Zahran pointed to the powder. "A miracle awaits."

"What is it?"

"The Cure."

"For the plague?"

"For plague and all ills."

Nigel felt his hopes slump once more. Jengo had mentioned something that would "save" his friends. Rachard had said the same a few moments ago. But a panacea…?

Riiiiight.

Zahran pulled a plastic bottle from below and shook out an empty gelatin capsule. He separated the halves, dipped them into the powder, then fitted them back together.

Nigel got a good look at the Mungu's hands during the process. They'd looked gnarled before but up close they were positively deformed, with bulbous finger joints that barely moved. The fact that he was able to fill the capsule was damn near miraculous in itself.

Somehow he managed to pinch it between a twisted thumb and a bent forefinger and proffer it to Nigel.

"For you."

"What's in it?"

"Life."

Uh-huh.

Rachard's comment came back to him: *Believers only, mon…*

"Why me?"

"Only good man dare flies to look for little boy he never met. After plague, the world need good men."

He handed Nigel a battered Evian bottle that apparently had undergone multiple refills – but from where? Though obviously missing a few gears, the Mungu seemed sincere in his desire to help. But no way Nigel was taking that pill and washing it down with that water.

He was reminded of the kid who handed you an unlabeled pill in the schoolyard. What is it? Good stuff, just take it. Nigel had given in once and wound up so sick he'd thought he was going to die.

"Is it okay if I save this for later? If I find my faith?" After he'd found Bandora he'd chuck it away. "I wouldn't want to insult your believers by taking it simply to please you."

"Wise as well as good," Zahran said, grinning. "All you need is to believe in God's grace and He will protect you."

Believe? he thought as he slipped the capsule into his pocket. You don't know what you're asking, mate.

As the thought of all his pointless rows with Abby hit home again, he gritted his teeth and tried to smile graciously. It didn't come naturally.

"Thank you. But I still need to find Bandora. Can't you give me any help – any help at all?"

Zahran gave his head a slow, sad shake. "I cannot. You will find him when you are ready." With unexpected agility, Zahran got to his feet, stepped to the tent flap and lifted it. "Go with God."

"But–" Nigel felt a hand grip his arm. Boynt was pulling him up. "Hey–"

"When the Mungu says go," Rachard said, "you go."

They escorted him back to the parking lot and left him at his car. He sat in the dark without starting the engine.

They were lying. All of them. Especially Zahran. He knew Bandora's exact whereabouts but wasn't telling. Why play these games though? Why hadn't they just shrugged off the picture and said they'd never seen the boy. Why did Nigel feel like he was being toyed with like a cat swats at a mouse before killing it?

Even more of a mystery was why they cared about the boy. None of his research had shown the Hakizimanas to be special in any way, so how could their son be special?

And yet apparently he was – special enough for his uncle to kidnap him and Zahran and his followers to lie about him.

MONDAY

NIGEL

Again Nigel slept later than usual.

He'd crawled into bed last night, sure he'd drop off immediately, but sleep hadn't come. Questions about that little boy and where he was and who was watching over him and how well they were taking care of him swirled about him until the wee hours.

Sunlight through the windows woke him. He kicked off the covers and sat on the edge of the bed, wondering about his next step.

Where the hell did he go from here?

With no answer to that, he grabbed the phone and called home.

"You all right?" he said after her hoarse hello.

Abby said, *"I think I caught a cold on top of everything else. How's it going down there?"*

"I've hit a wall."

He told her about meeting Zahran and his suspicions.

"Why would they want a little boy?"

"That's the million-dollar question, isn't it."

"You don't think they're... perverts or like that?"

"Honestly, I don't. If it's anything – and I could be totally wrong about them – it's got to be religious." He was tired of talking about Bandora. "How about you? You sound weak."

"Just this cold and my period making me feel a bit crappy."
"Any plans for the day?"
"Yeah. Vegetate."
"Good. You do that. Feel better. And stay inside. I'll call you later."
"I might be sleeping."
"Good. Sleep as much as you can. See you soon, I hope."

He ended the call and looked around the room. The TV was a waste of time, but his laptop sat hibernating on the desk. He jabbed the touchpad. The hard drive whirred and the screen lit with the Glastonbury Abbey video where he'd paused it. He got it running again and leaned back to watch.

The camera – from the poor resolution it had to be somebody's phone – began panning the crowd and its mix of black and white faces. As the shot cruised those up front by the pickup, it slowed as it caught a black guy with a bleached blond afro.

Nigel shot forward and hit the pause icon. The shot was blurry, but how many black guys with a white afro could be fans of Zahran? No question: He'd found Jengo. The guy had been standing right in front of Zahran that day. How could the Mungu say he didn't know him? Okay, Jengo could be just another nameless face in the crowd, but Nigel didn't think so.

He headed for the shower. Time for another visit to Abbey Park. If people hadn't seen the boy, they might have seen Jengo.

BBC:

Word from the United States that the President has canceled a press conference scheduled for this afternoon. Concern is growing about his health. The US Senate is calling a recess due to the inability to assemble a quorum of members. Many have returned to their homes or are not responding to calls. The House of Representatives called a similar recess two days ago.

NIGEL

Before heading to the abbey, Nigel cruised the town, looking for an open store. Not many to choose from. As he turned onto Market Place he saw a man come out of a little Co-Op. Okay, something was open. He stopped and dashed inside. Like almost every other little shop in every other tourist town these days, it sold ski masks and balaclavas along with its maps and sunglasses and postcards.

Apparently his red-and-blue striped model was now well known among the mungu mob, so he'd need something new to wear. He bought a brand new black one. He pulled it on and checked himself in the mirror on the sunglasses rack. Perfect. He looked like an IRA Provisional, just like everyone else. The day was bright so he bought a pair of sunglasses to hide his eyes as well. He was starting to feel almost optimistic about finding Bandora. What happened after that…

He wanted to buy a cola but the cooler was empty.

At Abbey Park he parked where he had before and began wandering the tent city. He figured maybe a hundred tents in all, but not laid out in any sort of order. Just set down wherever they damn well pleased.

He started out trying to look casual, like he was simply getting some exercise, but that didn't permit the kind of search he needed to do. So he switched gears and became a man looking for his dog.

This allowed him to stop at closed tents and make inquiries: *My girlfriend's dog's run off. Yeah, a little Yorkie, answers to the name of "Buttons." He's a royal pain in the arse but my girl loves him and I won't know a moment's peace until he's found.*

Most of the people he spoke to were young, couples and groups of friends in their twenties and thirties, dressed in jeans and scruffy tops, mainly hippie and rave style, but here and there he found older people, those who not so long ago had sensible white-collar jobs. Seemed that a need for hope was not exclusive to the youth who would normally be camped around here to get high and listen to their favorite bands before heading back to Uni and whatever sober future awaited them. They were all polite. None of them had seen his dog.

Using the two towering remnants of what he assumed was once the entrance to the Abbey or a cathedral of sorts as landmarks, he worked his way east and west. He was half way through a winding, eastward trek, heading toward those tall ruins, when he spotted a bareheaded man crossing what would have been the nave if the church still had a roof. He wore a sweater and slacks, but even at this distance, Nigel knew that face. He couldn't believe it. Not again.

Singh!

Nigel charged. He wasn't getting away this time. But he didn't have a clear course to run. People cluttered the path, making him dodge and weave and stutter and even stop once. When he reached the ruin Singh was nowhere in sight.

Nigel gave into an angry dance, then pulled it together and headed back to the tents. He was shaking inside. He did not – *not* – believe in ghosts, but either he'd seen fucking Rajiv Singh walking through that ruined church, or he was going off the deep end of guilt, or someone was gas-lighting him and doing a damn fine job of it.

Except for the skin. This was the first time he'd seen the – what? – apparition in full daylight and his skin had looked strange. Tight and almost shiny, like a mask.

Well, Singh was dead and Nigel couldn't imagine who'd go to the trouble to spook him, so it had to be in his head. He was hallucinating. That wasn't like him. He wasn't neurotic and had pretty much stopped thinking about the Singhs.

Was that it? He'd replaced the Singhs with Bandora and his subconscious wasn't having any of it? He didn't like it one bit, but that was the only answer that made sense.

He made his way back to the tents and resumed his search, his sunglasses keeping the folks around him from knowing where he was looking. He kept up the *Here-Buttons-Buttons-Buttons* chant as he peeked into tents that had a flap open and poked his head into any that didn't. He ran into some hostility when he surprised someone inside, but the lost dog story smoothed things over.

He was about three-quarters of the way through when he poked his head inside a closed tent – little more than a pup tent, really – and saw a blond afro sticking out of a sleeping bag. Yes! Had to be Jengo. His heart raced. At fucking last.

He did a quick survey of the tiny space – no sign of Bandora, but in the corner was a small, worn cuddly bunny rabbit and a bright children's picture book shoved in a bag. Nigel didn't need any more to know that Bandora had been with him. Where was he now? He flinched as he leaned inside. It stank in here much worse than Zahran's tent. Reminded him of–

Oh, hell! The Hakizimana house.

As he entered in a crouch and knelt beside the bedroll, he noticed it was soaked through with sweat and piss and less pleasant fluids. Jengo lay on his left side, facing away. Nigel rolled him onto his back and groaned when he saw the glazed eyes and sunken cheeks.

End-stage plague.

He shook his shoulder. "Jengo!" He kept his voice low. "Jengo!"

This close up, Nigel could see no dark roots in his blond afro. Was his hair really white? He kept shaking him till he focused – sort of.

"Whuh?" His voice sounded like a shoe scuffing slate.

"Where's Bandora?" No comprehension. "Bandora! Your nephew, dammit! Bandora!"

His face screwed up and he sobbed. "Ban... Mungu..." He mumbled something in a language Nigel didn't understand.

"English, dammit! *English!*"

Nigel must have got through to him because he whispered, "Old Way...Old Way."

The dopers had mentioned that too.

"What's 'Old Way'?" He shook him harder. "Jengo! What's 'Old Way'?"

Instead of answering, he said, "He comes! God comes!"

Nigel wanted to throttle him. He remembered the Hakizimanas crying out that they didn't deserve to see god. Why? Because they'd trusted their boy would be safe in the company of his uncle?

"Real or not, you don't deserve that, you son of a bitch! What's 'Old Way'? Tell me, goddamnit! Where's Bandora?"

Jengo opened his mouth to speak but stiffened instead as the air caught in his throat with a harsh click, then he went limp.

Nigel tried more shaking but no use. Jengo Hakizimana, the rotten fucker who'd kidnapped his nephew for reasons unknown, was gone. Nigel rose and crouched over him, resisting the urge to kick the dead son of a bitch.

Okay. Time to call some attention to this and rattle a cage or two. He stepped outside the tent – Christ, the fresh air smelled good – and began shouting.

"Hey, there's a dead man here! Died of the plague! Dead man here!"

HENRY

He approached Tower Bridge from the south. When he reached it he found he had the west pedestrian walk all to himself. The east was equally deserted. Well, really, what idiot would be out for a stroll at midday? The rare car on the bridge slowed to gawk as it passed.

I must be a right pretty sight, he thought.

Being starkers except for a pair of goggles would be enough alone to draw looks, but before setting out a mile or so back, he'd used a trowel to coat himself from head to toe with a mixture of super-sticky glue and his own blood. Everywhere but his eyelids. He needed to see and the goggles protected his vision. Then he'd begun walking, pushing a pram loaded with two thirty-pound dumbbells and two pairs of handcuffs.

He'd left Jamie sick at home. Alex was dead. And along the way Henry had realized how quickly London was breaking down. Almost every alley he passed contained a rotting corpse or two – people with the plague who'd thought they could survive one more trip in search of food but didn't make it back. Instead of being carted off for burial or burning, they'd been left where they fell to rot and breed more flies.

And oh, the flies. The blood-glue mix had done just what he'd hoped: The little flies caught the scent and flocked to him. Millions of them, it seemed, swarming in for a bite. But when they landed on him they stayed – couldn't bite, couldn't leave. Their furious, frustrated buzzing was music, a symphony. Soon he was totally coated, head to toe, with the little fuckers. Even his cock. They wanted to suck blood from his cock. Did that make them cocksuckers? It sure as hell did. He let out a laugh. A madman's cackle.

Yes, what a sight he must be. A man of flies pushing a pram within a cloud of flies.

Not to worry, folks. No baby in here. I'll never harm another child. I'm done with harming anything but flies.

He stopped midspan and leaned against the wooden rail along the top of the safety wall. It rose only to the bottom of his chest and he crushed a few hundred flies in the leaning. No worry. More where they came from. Plenty more.

The off-center glass egg of City Hall squatted to his left, while the Gherkin dominated the north bank on the right. He'd heard people bitch about both buildings, but he liked the Gherkin. Reminded him of a sleek spaceship ready to rocket to the stars. Directly below, the Thames flowed as it always had, unmindful of the plague.

Henry took a deep breath. Time to do this.

He pulled a pair of cuffs from the pram and snapped one of the bracelets around his left wrist. Then he fastened the second pair around his right. Next he snapped the free bracelet on each around the shaft of a dumbbell. Then, gripping a weight in each hand, he sat atop the railing and crushed another thousand flies on his butt as he settled there with his legs dangling over the water.

A car behind him began to honk. Trying to get him to stop or egging him on? Henry didn't know, didn't care. Nobody was going to get out and try to stop a fly-coated man. Maybe they wanted to call out to him, but that meant lowering a window. No-no. Might let death into the car.

He was on his own. But then, he'd been on his own since Maggie and Livvy passed, hadn't he.

He looked down at the gray water flowing not so far below. He'd feared it unlikely that the fall would be enough to kill him and he didn't trust himself not to fight the undercurrents and try and swim for the banks when panic gripped him. Thus the sixty pounds of lead locked to his wrists. He'd go under and stay under.

"Little Singh girl!" he shouted. God, he didn't even know her name. "I'm sorry!" Then, "Maggie! Livvy! I'm on my way!"

He slipped off the ledge and plummeted toward the water.

And I'm taking a million of these fuckers with me.

NIGEL

He felt like he'd gone back in time, transplanted into the fourteenth century as a cart driver. Only the cart was Zahran's pickup and Rachard wasn't crying "Bring out your dead," but the Black Death parallel was inescapable.

Rachard had shown up at Jengo's tent wearing only a T-shirt and jeans, seeming more surprised to find Nigel there than Jengo dead.

"You back then?"

Nigel had let the obviousness pass. "This is the guy I've been looking for."

Rachard had shrugged. "Some die. Ja's will, mon."

He'd brought the pickup and Nigel helped him load Jengo's body into the open rear bed. Not wanting to lose the opportunity to question Rachard some more, Nigel took the wheel, driving him around the perimeter of the tent city. Rachard would call out, "We're heading for the moors!" until someone would wave. Then they'd load another body into the back. When they'd gathered half a dozen, Rachard slipped into the passenger seat and pointed west.

"That way."

"Where are we going?"

He pointed again. "Their final resting place, mon."

Soon they were out of Glastonbury and onto narrow country roads. Nigel realized these were the moors he could see from the rear of Meare Manor. To the left and right – more to the right – he saw pockets of dark haze about a hundred meters or so off the road.

"What're those?"

Rachard didn't seem to need to look to know what Nigel was talking about. 'Resting places.'

Nigel didn't get it but he sensed more questions would yield no more details. It grew hot in the cab so Rachard rolled down his window and stripped off his T-shirt.

"You're not worried about the flies?"

Rachard's dreads waved like tentacles as he shook his head. "No, mon. I took the Cure."

The cure…right.

Nigel jerked a thumb over his shoulder at the dead in the truck bed. "Why weren't they given it?"

"They were. All Zahran's followers partake."

Nigel shook his head to clear it. Was he missing something here?

"They're not looking very cured to me."

"They lacked faith, mon. Y'gotta have faith in the Mungu for the Cure to work. If you don't, you wind up like them."

"Then it's not really a cure."

More religious crap. Everywhere, and growing stronger as the plague took hold.

Rachard smiled. "Oh, but mon, it is. Ja is casting a wide net, collecting the righteous with the wicked and sorting them out when they come to Him. The Mungu brings the word of Ja to the people. If you have faith that Ja speaks through the Mungu, the Cure will let you live on to hear the Mungu."

Nigel gathered that "Ja" was god. But as for the Cure...

"So much for a panacea."

Rachard frowned. "What?"

"A cure-all."

"But I am cured. I used to have headaches and backaches, and now I have none." He spread his bare arms. "All fruits ripe."

Most probably psychosomatic, Nigel thought. Placebo effect.

"Congrats."

"And you?" Rachard said. "The Mungu gave you the Cure. You taken it yet?"

"Maybe later. I need to find the boy first. Maybe that will give me some faith in something. You do this job often? You picked up any kids killed by the plague?

"No. No children." They were approaching an intersection about eight kilometers west town. Rachard said, "Make right here."

Nigel did as instructed, biting back his frustration. Maybe this was a waste of his time. Rachard wasn't a talker, that was for sure. They followed a bumpy dirt road until he was directed to turn right again onto a path that consisted of little more than two ruts.

"Where the hell are we going?" Nigel said as they bumped along.

"Almost there."

A hundred meters later Rachard raised a hand. "Here is good. Time to unload." He hopped out of the cab. When Nigel didn't move, he said, "Come on, mon. You gotta help."

Together they dropped the tailgate and began unloading the bodies one by one. Rachard took the feet, leaving Nigel up with the arms as they moved the bodies to a grassy spot maybe ten meters off to the side of the road. Rachard was meticulous about their placement, directing each be laid three feet apart with face up, head north, feet south.

When all six – four women and two men were laid out – Nigel stepped back and said, "Now what? Sorry, but I didn't sign on as gravedigger."

He didn't want to be outside any longer than he had to.

Rachard's dreads swung again with the quick shake of his head. "No worry, mon."

He went back to the truck and returned with a machete.

Oh, shit, Nigel thought, freezing at sight of its honed black blade. "What–?"

Without a word, Rachard stepped up beside one of the bodies and slashed at it, opening the belly from sternum to pubes.

Nigel stumbled back, almost tripping and falling in his haste and revulsion. "For God's sake!"

"Exactly," Rachard said.

He then used the tip of the machete to part the incision, letting glistening coils of intestine push through.

He then moved to the second, Jengo's lifeless body, and did the same. Nigel watched in gaping horror as he repeated the process on all six corpses.

"What the fuck!" was all he could say, over and over.

"They did not make a home for belief while they were alive." Rachard said as he wiped the blade on the grass. "So now they make homes for new flies."

Nigel now understood the pockets of dark haze across the moor: clouds of flies over the final resting places of the partially eviscerated remains of belief-challenged followers of Zahran.

A fly buzzed by and landed on the exposed intestines of one of the corpses. Then another.

"Let's get out of here."

Rachard smiled at him. "Nuh haste, mon."

He started for the pickup. "Easy for you to say."

"Cu ya!"

He turned to see Rachard holding up his forearm and pointing at the fly that had landed on it. Instinctively Nigel raised his gloved hand to slap it away.

"No, do not!" Rachard said. "I partook of the Cure. And I have faith."

Sweat leaking from every pore, Nigel watched Rachard flinch as the fly took a bite out of his skin. Seconds later the fly took off on his own. Rachard grinned as he displayed the tiny droplet of blood where he had been bitten.

"See? No worry."

Shaking his head, Nigel jumped back into the truck and started the engine.

The lunatics were running the asylum.

ABBY

Abby ended the call and sagged into a chair. Nigel's second of the day. She couldn't remember the last time he'd called twice in one day. She'd managed to sound cheerful enough, she thought. At least she hoped so.

He, on the other hand, had sounded so down, as if he'd lost all hope of finding that little boy. She'd fought the urge to tell him to hurry home so she could hold him and assure him everything was all right.

But he'd know right away she wasn't, wouldn't he? Soon as he stepped through that door he'd know she was dying.

Forty-eight hours since the bites and she felt utterly deflated. This morning, before her strength had faded, she'd slid the comfy chair over near the bathroom door and stacked water bottles on the floor next to it. The only food left was canned but not an issue because the uremia from forgoing dialysis had sapped her appetite. But she knew she'd be thirsty.

She might not be able to answer the phone tomorrow, so she'd told Nigel she was going to the hospital for a volunteer shift. He didn't want her out of the house but she'd said her mind was made up.

Am I doing the right thing? she thought for the thousandth time since Nigel had left.

She had no doubts about allowing herself to be bitten, or about skipping the dialysis – her feet were firm and confident on that path – and none about the dying itself. But dying alone, without Nigel… without his even knowing. Was that right? Would he feel betrayed?

She shook herself. Who was she kidding? Of course he would. She'd lied to him. She just hoped her explanation in the video she'd made yesterday would ease the hurt.

But no way she could have him here. He'd be dragging her to hospital and she'd be too weak to resist. Not that it would matter. The plague was in control now. She could tell by the pallor in her mirror. Her red cells were dissolving, melting away like snowflakes in a sunbeam.

She felt no pain, just a sick feeling in her stomach and exhaustion beyond imagining. She could still force herself to her feet and shuffle to the bathroom. But soon she wouldn't be able to do that. And then it would get messy. She hated the thought of anyone, especially Nigel, finding her like that.

No, she'd go to her Lord and Savior alone. By this time tomorrow she'd be basking in His glow as she waited for Nigel.

NIGEL

He was hungry so he wandered down to the dining room but found it deserted – no staff and no diners. He went to the front desk and rang the bell until the woman appeared from somewhere in the back.

"Aren't you serving dinner tonight?"

The woman behind the desk shook her head. "You're the only guest, sir. None of the staff showed up today."

"None? But my bed was made."

She gave him a sad smile. "I took care of that." Tears sprang into her eyes. "It's all falling apart, isn't it." It wasn't a question.

What could he say? He didn't have a spirit-lifting platitude to offer. And what would be the point of one anyway?

"I'm afraid it is. Look, do you mind if I root around in the kitchen and see if there's anything to eat? I'm famished."

"Oh, please help yourself."

"Do you want me to bring you anything?"

"No," she said, shaking her head. "I'm not hungry."

He noticed her pallor. "You look tired. Have you been...?"

"Bitten?" Her smile looked forced. "Not that I know of. But one doesn't always know, does one."

"I'm sure it's just stress. We're all feeling it."

At a loss for words, he hurried away.

The kitchen had large ovens. Looked like they did some of their own baking. He found some sliced ham, some bread that wasn't stale but on the way, and a jar of mustard. He threw together two sandwiches, grabbed a couple of bottles of beer from behind the bar, and sat at a table near the wall.

Strange to be the only one in the whole dining room. He felt like the last man on the *Titanic*. All the lifeboats were gone and he had no way of getting off, so what the hell, grab a sandwich and a beer. The metaphor for everything he was doing wasn't lost on him. Finding one child while the world died was equally ridiculous when he thought about it.

Not that he'd given up on living. Zahran's cure might be mumbo-jumbo bullshit, but scientists around the world would be working on a real one. He just had to stay safe until they found it.

He finished everything and bused his plates and bottles back to the kitchen. Then, enjoying his beer buzz, stepped out the back door for some fresh air. The sun was down so he didn't have to worry about covering up. His car and another – the receptionist's, he guessed – had the lot to themselves. He noticed his inside light was on.

How'd that happen? he wondered as he strolled toward it.

He was pretty sure no one had broken in. First off, nobody about, and he didn't have anything valuable inside. Didn't even bother to lock it most of the time.

He found the driver door ajar. He'd closed it, hadn't he? He couldn't remember. He'd been in quite a state when he'd got back… images of Rachard slitting those bellies open had been playing tag with close ups of that fly biting his arm.

Maybe he hadn't closed the door. Maybe he'd given it a push and it hadn't caught. Whatever the reason, good thing he'd stepped out because he might have found himself with a dead battery tomorrow, and fat chance of finding someone with cables to give him a jump.

As he pulled it open to give it a proper slam, something buzzed out of the interior and landed on his neck. He felt a sting and slapped at it.

"Oh, no!"

He'd crushed it against his skin. He grabbed it and kicked the car door shut, then ran for the hotel. Inside the back door he inspected it under the light. Half crushed with one leg still kicking, but no doubt about it: one of the African flies. No question.

"Shit!"

His stomach turned to water and then to ice. He wanted to rewind time. To skip dinner. To have stayed in his room. He threw the fly to the floor and ground it under his shoe.

"Shit-shit-shit!"

No. This couldn't be happening. He'd been so careful, and then to be bitten by a fucker trapped in his car? No. Couldn't be.

He ran up to his room and leaped to the bathroom mirror where he found a tiny little puncture.

No! Fuck no!

Frantic, he grabbed the soap and washcloth and scrubbed the area until his skin felt raw. He wasn't giving up yet. What else? He had no alcohol. How about–?

The pill – the Cure. Zahran's pill. Where had he put it? He slammed the wardrobe's sliding door aside and found his trousers on the shelf over the hangers and pawed through his pockets. Please God, don't let it have fallen out somewhere. Please.

"Gotta be here, gotta be–"

There. A gelatin cap filled with beige powder. He rushed to the sink, filled a glass from the tap, and washed it down without the slightest confidence that it would help.

Y'gotta have faith in the Mungu for the Cure to work. If you don't, you wind up like them...

Well, faith in the Mungo...he had no faith in that crazy African. Yet Nigel had seen him bitten by flies – thousands of them – and he was still walking around. And Rachard... one of those African flies had taken a bite out of him today. Nigel wished he'd asked him how many times he'd been bitten.

Maybe the Cure worked only for a minority who took it – some idiosyncratic internal effect countered the autoimmune reaction to the saliva. Maybe Nigel would be one of the lucky ones.

Yeah. Right.

He felt like crying. His skin crawled in panic.

"Shit-shit-*shit!*"

TUESDAY

NIGEL

He didn't know how he managed to fall asleep, but somehow he did, and he awoke feeling pretty good.

How was that possible? Too soon for symptoms? But all the research he'd done indicated that people became symptomatic within hours of an infected bite.

Zahran's pill?

No. He couldn't buy that. And yet...

Not only did he feel good, he was *hungry*. That had to be a good sign. A small wash of relief flooded through him and he wanted to laugh with elation. Maybe he was going to be all right after all.

He'd slept in his clothes so he simply straightened his shirt and tucked himself in. But before heading downstairs he called Abby. He wouldn't tell her about the fly bite. Even though he was fine, she'd only worry.

No answer...probably over at the hospital volunteering. They made you turn off your cell phone there. He'd try again later.

He headed downstairs and found the dining room still deserted. But so was the front desk. Was he the only one in the place?

After walking around calling out "Hello?" for about five minutes, he gave up and went to the kitchen. No eggs or orange juice about so he opted for another ham sandwich and coffee. Too creepy eating in the dining room with no one else in the building, so he carried the food up to his room. The TV was pretty much white static on all channels, and rather than sit in silence, once he'd eaten he called Mal to fill him in on his thus far not-so-fruitful search.

But when Mal answered, he knew something was wrong. His breathing sounded labored and it took him a long beat to manage a greeting.

"*Nigel. Good to hear you.*"

"Are you okay?"

"*No. I've got it. So does Amelia. A couple of flies got in the house and, well…*"

"Jesus, Mal. When?"

He almost told him about his own bite, but held back. He wasn't sure if it was out of care for his friend, or some kind of denial, but suddenly it seemed important that one of them be healthy.

"*If you're asking how much time I've got left, fuck knows. I'm not good. The whole paper seems to have come down with it. Toulson too.*"

Well, the news isn't all bad, he thought. No, don't be like that.

"Does he blame me for that too?"

"*He'd probably love to, but you wouldn't believe the flies here. The city's full of them. We've published our last edition, I'm afraid.*"

Typical Mal – headed for his deathbed but worrying about the paper.

"The *Light*'s gone out then?"

"*Afraid so. Did you find Bandora?*" A hint of urgency had crept in Mal's weakened voice.

"I haven't got him yet, but I think I know where he is." The lie came easily.

"*Really? You don't know how good that is to hear. I keep thinking about it. I'd like to know… before… if you know what I mean.*"

Before he died. Shit. This was surreal. Mal dying. Fuck, maybe he was too.

"I'll find him, Mal. Trust me."

"*Call me later?*"

"Sure. You rest."

Rest. Right. As if someone with the plague had a choice. As if resting was going to help any of them.

He drained his coffee, trying not to think about Mal's imminent death. Or his own bite. Instead he focused on Zahran and his riddles. The bastard knew something and it was time to find out what. He was going back and wasn't taking any bullshit this time.

He was already wearing jeans and a turtleneck, so he slipped on his ski mask and headed for the car park. He might have lucked out with that fly bite last night, but he wasn't taking chances.

Down in the otherwise empty lot, he made sure no other flies were waiting in his car, then got rolling. As he cruised through Glastonbury, even more deserted than yesterday, he kept his eye out for stray pedestrians, especially one who might be Indian. No Singh sighting this trip. No *anybody*.

He was halfway to the camp when the first symptoms hit him: muscle aches and nausea.

Aw, no. His face flushed with sudden panic and he squeezed the steering wheel. Maybe it was just the food. Maybe the ham had gone off. Maybe. But what were the odds? He gritted his teeth. Facts were his business. The sweat under his mask was telling him this was plague. *That* was the fact.

Through the windscreen the sun shone bright and clear on the countryside and he wanted to weep.

Three days after the bite. He had until Thursday.

Okay. Make the time mean something. The thought was a balm through the rush of fear that filled him. Get back to Abby, but finish the job first. For the Singhs, for Mal, and for his own sorry soul. He was so close… almost there.

He yanked the ski mask off and threw it angrily to one side. What could the flies do to him now?

At the Abbey he found the residents packing up, folding their tents and leaving their rubbish littering the ground.

"We're moving on," said a voice behind him. Boynt.

"Where to?"

"London. Westminster."

"Is Zahran taking the kid with him? Bandora?"

Another wave of nausea hit him as a reminder he no longer had time to fuck about.

"Forget about that boy."

"Where's the other half of your cheerful double act?"

"There." Boynt nodded toward a tent that no one was taking down, and then walked off toward an RV that already had its engine running.

Nigel leaned toward the closed flap.

"Rachard? You in there?"

"Who that be?" came a weak voice from within.

Nigel's stomach dropped. He lifted the flap and looked inside. Rachard lay on his back, looking… well, sick. He wouldn't be smoothing Nigel's path with Zahran, that was for sure.

"Oh, Christ. You've got it." *Too*, he almost added. His own infection still felt surreal.

"No, mon!" he said, frantically waving his hands. "I just got the miseries is all. Just the temporary miseries."

"I want to know where the boy is. You gonna tell me, or do I have to ask your crazy boss? I just want to get the boy and go home."

Rachard's eyes clouded. "Ask the Mungu."

"Just tell me."

Rachard turned onto his side, facing away. "You go now."

"Tell me, goddamnit! Did he catch the plague, is that it? Is he dead? Or is Zahran hiding him somewhere? Why?"

"Go. I need rest so I can follow the Mungu tomorrow."

Nigel's patience snapped. "You're not following him anywhere, you lying son of a bitch. You're a dead man and you know it."

Resisting the urge to kick down the tent, he turned and stepped out into the sunlight. Behind him, as the flap dropped back, he heard a wrenching sob and felt like a cunt.

But he needed to find that little boy and only one person could help. He walked toward the center of the camp and hoped that Zahran was still there.

He was.

His henchmen were loading his tent and meager possessions into the back of a white van – a mundane method of travel for a self-proclaimed spokesman for God – and the man himself was staring up at the sky, enjoying the sun on his face. The same sun was on Nigel's but it didn't stop him from wanting to strangle the man for his freedom in the world. For his days beyond the next three. His legs felt weak beneath him.

"Zahran."

The wizened head turned to him and, on seeing his exposed face, smiled. "You have found faith, I see."

Nigel stepped up close. "I think my mask is no longer required."

"Ah." Understanding dawned. "A bite." He shrugged. "You have the cure."

"I'm not holding out much hope."

"But you took?" He smiled again. Of course Nigel had taken it. Who wouldn't?

"All I want is to know what happened to the boy. If he's still alive. I'm not exactly a threat to you anymore."

Knowing the plague was wreaking its hell on his bloodstream stripped away the bullshit.

"Ah, Bandora. A special boy. Sacred child."

"So you *do* know him?" The tiredness creeping over him washed away. He was getting somewhere. "Why sacred? He's from an ordinary family."

"Jengo knew. He brought him to me."

"What did he know?" Nigel wanted to shake the old man until he rattled.

"The old ways." He stared at Nigel. "Look at your picture again."

Infuriated, Nigel unfolded the sheet and stared.

"What?"

"You see, but you don't see." A melodic tone. It jarred against the thrum of the van's diesel engine starting up. "This is not photograph. Just drawing. No light." A pause. "No color."

Nigel looked again. No color. He thought of Jengo's blonde hair. He remembered how Bandora's parents had kept him hidden. Pieces of the jigsaw moved slowly together.

"He's an albino?"

"A sacred child. A gift from God."

Someone inside the van whistled. They were ready to get moving.

"Please. Where is he? Is he alive? I need to know."

"He lives," Zahran said. "He lives in *you.*' He waved an arm at the dismantling tent city. "He lives in all of them."

"What the hell does that mean?" Sounded like one of Abby's religious rants.

"I told you that you and the boy would find each other when ready. The fly bite you. You take the cure. You and the boy are united."

The cure. Bandora was the cure. The crushed powder in the pestle and mortar. A little boy's bones.

As Nigel reeled, Zahran stepped away and climbed into the van. "God bless you."

Tires moved on the mud. Nigel barely heard them past the rushing in his head. His stomach twisted and he threw up, nearly falling to his knees. As he gasped for breath and let his stretched muscles recover, the awful truth settled.

He'd heard stories before while on his travels, mentions in the London papers a few years ago. Albino murders in Tanzania, hacked to death and their bones crushed up and used by witch doctors for fake cures.

Shit. Shit. He wanted to cry all over again. He'd taken the cure. He'd come to save the boy and he was now a part of his destruction, and dying of the plague to boot.

He wiped snot from his face and dragged himself back to the car. Mal was waiting for a call. What the hell was he going to tell him?

The car meandered its way back to the hotel. Good thing he had both lanes to himself. His hands trembled and his head thumped loudly and he was grateful when he abandoned the machine in the car park and staggered through the empty reception area. Vomiting had made him weaker and he worked up a sweat climbing the stairs to the second floor. He collapsed on the unmade bed for a moment to catch his strength.

Less than three days left if he was lucky. The last chance at some kind of redemption had vanished when he'd swallowed that capsule. He didn't know whether to scream or to cry.

He needed to talk to Abby. He wouldn't tell her about the bite until he got home – he'd leave right away before the symptoms got worse – but he needed to hear her voice.

No answer.

Worry nibbled at him. Where was she? At the hospital? Seemed like an awful long time. Had she gone to church maybe? He wanted her inside. Where she'd be safe. His eyelids felt heavy, but he didn't put the phone down. He had another call to make and then he'd try Abby again.

He dialed Mal. It rang for over a minute before he answered. His breathing was a rattle. How long ago had he been bitten?

"Mal?"

"*Did you find him? Is he okay?*" Every word sounded like an effort.

"Yes. Yes, I found him."

"*And is he...?*"

The ache in the unfinished question down the line stabbed at Nigel. How could he tell Mal what had happened to his wife's relative? What did he have left? A day? Less? He thought of the only gift he had left for anyone and the irony of it: dishonesty.

"He's fine. He's sleeping. Jengo's dead, but this Zahran had kind of adopted him."

"*He's not been bitten?*"

"No. And I've got him totally wrapped up. I'll take him home with me to Abby later."

He blinked back tears that stung the back of his eyes. No happy ending was ever real.

"*Good. Good. Will you...I know it's a lot to ask, but...*" The line was starting to crackle slightly.

"We'll look after him Mal. I promise you."

"*Thank you, Nigel. You don't know how much this means. We can...*
we can relax now. Thanks."

"See you soon, Mal."

The line went dead. After a moment he ran to the bathroom
and threw up again.

BBC:

<no transmission>

NIGEL

The vomiting seemed to magnify all his symptoms. He collapsed
on the bed and lay there staring at the ceiling. Finally he roused
himself and tried to call Abby again but couldn't raise her. He looked
at his phone display and saw *NO SERVICE* on the screen.

Brilliant. Had the local towers gone dead?

He had to get home. He sat up and felt the room tilt. He held on
and it righted itself. But when he tried to stand it went into a spin
and his knees gave out. He gave it a moment then crawled back onto
the bed. He needed rest. He'd just close his eyes for a few minutes,
then he'd try again...

ABBY

At some point Abby had hauled herself downstairs to lay on the
sofa. She no longer cared about water or thirst; her body was way
beyond that being an issue. Why she hadn't gone to bed, she didn't
know. It would have been more comfortable – more natural. To die
in bed, that was what everyone wanted, wasn't it? To slip peacefully
away. Maybe not this young. And maybe not like this. Whatever, she
had ended up on the sofa, sprawled out and sweating, the cushions
beneath her soaking from her escaping water and chilling her skin
through her wet clothes.

Her phone was tossed, useless, on the carpet. The battery had
died at some point, and the last time she'd tried it – a moment of
wanting to hear Nigel's voice for one last time – the networks had
been down anyway.

Night had fallen as she lingered in her haze, but she didn't mind. The dark would be all the better for seeing the light of God when He came. Surely that must be soon. Time had drifted. She was pretty sure this was day three, even though the past 24 hours had seemed endless. She was at death's door, she knew that, her body was screaming it at her – or perhaps more like whimpering it at her, she had so little energy left – so where was He?

Had she done the right thing? She'd been so sure and now doubt was creeping in. If she hadn't, if God frowned on her for allowing herself to be bitten, He might not come.

No. Faith. Have faith. That was what this was all about.

All she could do was wait. Her limbs were too heavy to move, as if her body was rehearsing for the stillness of the grave. Her eyelids ached to sink closed forever, but she forced herself to blink. To stay awake. She wanted to see Him when he came for her. She had nothing else left.

She drifted some more, and then suddenly… light. A vague, darting beam. Her heart raced, the last of her physical strength joining her spiritual hope. Was this it? Was He finally coming for her?

Her vision was blurry, the world out of focus from sickness, and the light grew closer until it was so bright she had to squint. She gasped and smiled and croaked a laugh. God. At last she would see His face. Nothing else mattered.

"Mrs. Thompson?"

The light wavered. She hadn't expected God to speak. And the accent. What was that? Indian? Pakistani?

He repeated her name, and she tried to murmur a response. She tried to focus. Why was God using her married name? It didn't make sense. It didn't…

Suddenly the overhead lights came on and she groaned as the world became clear. Not God at all. An Indian man holding a torch leaned over her. She wanted to cry.

The man threw the torch to the carpet and pulled a bottle of water from his jacket pocket. He tipped some carefully between her lips. She was too weak to do anything but swallow.

"I'm here to help you," he said. "You are not going to die."

"Who are you?" she finally whispered.

"A doctor. My name is Singh." He paused and gently pushed her sweaty hair out of her eyes. "I have been following your husband."

"Doctor Singh?" she said. The haze was gripping her again. But that was… wasn't he dead? How could he be…? And then the blackness came, no light of God in it, no light at all, and she passed out into oblivion.

WEDNESDAY

ABBY

The light that woke her was brilliant sunshine. She lay in bed and a warm breeze moved through the room from the open window. Somewhere a fly buzzed. A perfect summer's day. For a moment, the fever, the sickness, the plague itself seemed like the echo of a dream. Then the ache in her parched throat hit her and her head throbbed.

The man. She hauled herself up to a half-sitting position. Her arms trembled with the effort, but she couldn't deny that although she still felt monumentally shit, the crisis had passed. She should be dead. She knew that. She'd been dying. She'd had the plague. So what the hell had happened? This was day four. There should be no day four. She should have been with God now.

Footsteps came up the stair. The clink of crockery. Her heart leapt as a shadow fell across her door. Nigel? Was he home?

"I thought you might be hungry," said an unfamiliar voice. "You should try to eat."

A stranger. That man. Singh. The fevered dream of last night came back to her. A doctor Singh, but not the ill-fated one Nigel's faulty research had named as root of the plague. Couldn't be. He looked similar, but something about the man's skin made him look as if he had survived a fire. It looked stretched and shiny, almost a

149

varnished look, reminding her of photos of Hollywood stars' facelifts gone wrong.

He placed the tray – a bowl of baked beans and rice, topped with tinned tuna alongside a pot of tea – and then retreated to a respectable distance.

"Eat. Please. An unusual breakfast, I know, but all I could find in your cupboards were tins and–"

"Who are you and why are you here?"

Her voice was stronger. Another betrayal of her soul by her body. Her stomach rumbled, but she refused to touch the food until he told her what he was doing in her house. "How did you get in? What do you want?"

"I am Ganek Singh. My brother was Rajiv Singh and–"

She started, pushing herself back against the headboard and almost spilling the tray. "Oh, God!"

"I mean you no harm."

Fear had an icy grip on her throat. "Where's my husband? Where's Nigel?"

"He is in Glastonbury. I followed him there."

"Why? Is he all right? Have you… hurt him?"

"I did him no harm."

That was a relief. But…

"Then why–?"

"I returned to find you. I saw you sick through the window and getting in was easy. There are no police to chase burglars."

"Things are that bad?"

"Everyone is sick." He looked at her and then shrugged. "Nearly everyone. Eat your food."

His tight, shiny face was impassive and if she wasn't so damned tired she'd want to punch him. She was supposed to be dead. How had he cured her? He had no right. Even if she'd somehow survived the plague she should be feeling the effects of going without her dialysis so long.

"What have you done to me?"

"We can talk more on the road." He moved back to the doorway. "But you will need some energy."

"Road to where?" she called after him, but he was already out of the room.

A few moments later she heard the pipes gurgle as water ran in the kitchen. He was washing up. Normality in the midst of chaos. She stared at the food through eyes stinging with tears and her body relinquished its bitterness at living and raged with hunger. She dug into the rice and beans. What else was there to do?

———

Two hours later, when she'd managed to shower and dress, she climbed into the Range Rover parked outside and slumped in the passenger seat.

The food had given her energy and she had to admit she was feeling much better. Physically, at least. Emotionally and mentally she was exhausted. She'd been so *ready*. That had been taken from her. The only reason she'd got out of the house was that Singh – who swore he hadn't treated her in any way other than to give her some water and carry her upstairs to bed – said he would take her to Nigel and give her some explanation for what was going on with her.

They drove through the silent city with the windows open. Bodies lay in the street and flies – of all varieties – buzzed around them. Most houses had their curtains closed. London had become a graveyard, one that was taunting Abby by excluding her.

She closed her eyes and leant back against the headrest, trying desperately not to enjoy the warmth of the sun on her face. She'd asked before but had to ask again.

"You haven't hurt Nigel, have you?"

"My brother and his family died because of him. And perhaps, yes, I had vengeance in my heart when I followed him. I wanted to cause him pain, as he caused such pain for my family." He sighed, a long breath on the passing breeze. "But I am not a man given to such things by nature, and when I watched his search for the boy my heart softened. He is not a bad man."

"No," she said. "Pig-headed, stubborn, and occasionally stupid, but never bad." She opened her eyes, a rush of love for her husband – anticipation at seeing him - surprising her. "It wasn't his fault, you know. He will always believe it was, but it wasn't."

Along the hard shoulder of the motorway, cars were dotted at crazy angles where drivers had pulled over – giving up on their journeys and their fight against the plague. The air buzzed around them. Flies everywhere. How fast they had claimed England.

"He's been bitten, hasn't he?"

She didn't look at Singh. What other reason could he have for taking her to Nigel rather than Nigel coming back with him to her? Speaking the words aloud, a deadened statement, made them more surreal. Nigel wasn't supposed to get the plague – *she* was.

"I think so, yes."

The wheels turned endlessly under them and the engine hummed.

"I was bitten three times," she said, glancing down at her bare arm. "So why the fuck aren't I dead?" She spat out the words, accusing, venomous. "I should be with God now. I should be waiting for my husband."

"I too was bitten. I too survived."

"How? You're the doctor. Explain it. Just luck?" *Bad* luck. "Are we two in a million?"

"You see my skin?" He turned to face her and the sun danced off the strange smooth tightness. "Before the plague I had scleroderma. Then I was bitten. One of the first in England. Like you, I got sick. Thought I was dying. Being a surgeon, I knew there was nothing the hospital could do for me, so I stayed at home to die. But after the third day I recovered. Scleroderma, like systematic lupus, is an autoimmune disease. The hemolytic anemia of the plague is also an autoimmune disease. My theory is that one somehow counter-acts the other. The changes my condition caused prior to the plague are still there, but it has not progressed. The plague arrested it."

"But the lupus aside, I'm way overdue on my dialysis."

Abby was determined to keep a grip on death for as long as possible. Maybe she was just having a brief respite. Maybe her wellness was a temporary illusion.

"I think perhaps the second autoimmune reaction partially reversed the first. I have saliva again, and tears – I discovered that when Rajiv died. Without testing your blood, I would hazard a guess that your kidneys are functioning again. Not one hundred percent – I doubt they'll ever reach that level – but well enough to survive without dialysis."

"You're saying they're getting better?"

"I'm only saying *improved*."

Abby stared at him. Twenty-four hours ago she'd been expecting death. And now he was telling her that not only had she survived the plague but her lupus had been arrested.

"This is ridiculous. You're crazy."

"No. No, this is scientific. We aren't unique. The man your husband tracked to Glastonbury – this Zahran who thinks he's been chosen by his god – I saw him. His hands. It's clear he had rheumatoid arthritis. Another autoimmune disease."

"Just spit out what you're trying to tell me. In plain English."

"The irony of the plague is that people who have been chronically ill – like you and I and Zahran – are going to get well, and the healthy are going to die. So many of them. All of them." He stared intently at her. "For those of us left behind it will be like walking out of Africa again."

Left behind. Abby's heart thumped against her chest and she frowned as she stared out at the passing fields, desperate to find some purpose in it.

"Why wouldn't He choose the healthy?" she muttered. "Why such a clean division? It doesn't make sense."

Here and there fires burned in fields, an echo of the fires destroying cattle at the height of the foot-and-mouth outbreak, but this time human bodies blazed, those who were still alive trying to protect themselves by creating pyres of the dead.

"He?"

"God. They all see God when they die. He comes to take them. He's *saving* them."

"Vishnu comes to them?"

"No…*God*. The one true god."

Singh smiled slightly. "Oh, you mean Shiva? Or do you mean Brahma?"

"The *Christian* God."

"Humans have invented many gods. Why is yours the one now getting all the glory?"

"Because mine invented *us*." She wasn't going to have this argument. Not again. "And He's now judging us. That's why the chosen get the visions."

"You mean the hallucinations just before death. The light? That is not god. That is the result of hypoxia in the visual cortex. The 'vision' is given shape by the fading consciousness. If you think you'll see god, then that's what you'll see. It has become the last hope of the dying. A shared hallucination."

"You can think what you want." Abby turned her head away from him and sipped from her water bottle. "I know what I believe."

She waited for him to fight her, try and beat her down with his supposed logic like Nigel would. But he wasn't Nigel. Instead he stayed quiet for a few minutes before speaking. His words were soft.

"I shall respect your beliefs. But you should not be sad to be alive. If you believe in an all-powerful god, then that disrespects his will. Perhaps you are looking at it wrong. Perhaps he is not judging, but wishes to start again. Perhaps he is only trusting the strong to that task. Those who understand suffering already."

It was Abby's turn not to speak. Perhaps he had a point.

NIGEL

Mal would be dead now. Soon he'd be following him. Him and pretty much everyone else on this sorry planet. Who would be left? Zahran preaching his craziness at Westminster to a churchful of corpses. What would he do when the final follower died? Kill himself, Nigel hoped. End the whole sorry mess.

His life wasn't exactly flashing before him, but his mind was drifting back through the years, revisiting bits and pieces that until now he'd lost with the hurlyburly of actually living.

His first day on the paper. His wedding day. Sneaking out of the reception for twenty minutes with Abby and giggling while they fucked in the toilet, her long wedding dress pushed up around her waist. Appendicitis when he was ten, coming on fast after football and his mum telling him it was just tummy ache. The fear on her face after the operation.

All the yesterdays merged in his head as he drifted in and out of consciousness. He knew he should eat something, or drink something but the idea of trying to lift himself off the bed was too much to contemplate and no one had come to see if he was okay or tell him that he was overdue on his check out. Had they left? He couldn't remember hearing a car, but that was no guarantee. Perhaps the mother and her boy were somewhere else in the hotel, gazing at the ceiling, and feeling too weak to move.

With supreme effort he turned his head and gazed out the window. The sky was a perfect vivid blue, and the small wisps of clouds were like surf on the sea. Abby. Dorset. A weekend in July. More memories. He let them blur and closed his eyes. Sleep for a bit. Sleep would be good.

————

"Nigel? Nigel? Oh god."

"Let me see him."

A hand on his head. A pulse check. Eyelids being dragged open.

"How bad is it? Oh god. Can't you do something?"

Crying. Who was crying?

"Oh god."

"He is very sick. I'm sorry. A day more I think... that's all."

Nigel's consciousness finally broke surface.

"Man," he croaked. "I could have told you that."

And then Abby was on him, her hair across his face and her wet tears warm on the cold sweat that soaked his shirt. Abby. Abby was here. With all his energy, he lifted one arm and wrapped it round her. She was wearing a thin cotton shirt, no balaclava, no jacket, no gloves. She was with the man who'd been following him. He too was unprotected. For a brief moment his journalistic mind attempted to question it all, and then he realized that none of it mattered.

"The sea, Abs," he whispered into her sweet, soft hair. "I want to see the sea."

————

Nigel could feel the sunlight, taste the brine on the breeze, hear the sea somewhere out there before him, but could not see it. He'd caught a beautiful glimpse when he forced his lids open for a second as they'd placed his stretcher on the gentle incline of a dune, but couldn't find the will for another try.

Although he'd been slipping in and out of consciousness all day, he knew that Rajiv Singh's brother had gone to borrow an ambulance. Why not? No one else was using it. And then he and Abby – *glorious healthy Abby* – had loaded him in the back and headed west until they reached the sea. Then they carried him on a stretcher to the beach.

I'm dying, he thought. These are my last hours. Where's the panic?

Dying. Death. Nothing. That was what waited for him. All the life he'd led had come to this, and now it felt as if it had all been wisps of a dream left to flutter in this one moment. Final hours. No more tomorrows.

Maybe he was too weak to panic. He felt oddly at peace with the world, a peace he'd never known while up and about and healthy and death was something that happened to someone else. He was going away and what was left of the world would carry on without him. Just as well. He was so very, very tired.

Abby sat on his right and held his hand. Her palm was soft and warm and felt a million miles away. Singh sat on his left and did not hold his hand, thank you. *Small mercies.*

"I saw bags of IV fluid in the ambulance," Abby said, softly. "Can't we…?"

Their conversation washed over him like a breeze. He didn't like the pain in her voice.

It's okay, Abs. I'm a shit. I've been a shit for a long time. This ending could be shittier for someone like me.

Rajiv Singh had burned. His wife and little girl had burned. They'd died in terror and screaming. Yes, Nigel deserved worse than being carried out to death gently like driftwood on the sea.

Bandora. He didn't want to think about Bandora.

"Hook him up? Not a good idea."

Singh this time. Calm. Steady. A doctor. Even in all the madness of the plague he'd managed to wangle a doctor at his deathbed.

"But he's got to be dehydrated."

"A little. Not such a bad thing in his case. It concentrates the few red blood cells he has left. If we put a liter or two into him, the dilution will only worsen his hypoxia. And hypoxia is what's going to… carry him off. Not dehydration."

Abby's voice was barely audible. "Carry him off…"

In the ensuing silence Nigel again wondered at his calm acceptance of being "carried off."

The sun set, the air cooled, and he heard talk of taking him back to the ambulance for shelter. He managed to raise the energy to speak.

"No. Please. Stay here."

They didn't argue. He heard them building a fire from driftwood, then felt its heat as it caught. Light from the flames flickered through his closed lids. He felt as if he were in the dark, listening to a stereo audiobook. A clink of a bottle. Wine? He didn't blame her.

"It's got to make you laugh a bit, Nigel," Abby said, still on his right, clutching his hand. "You're going to get to see God and I'm not. Not yet."

Don't bet the savings account on that, Abs. It's a void. A nothing.

Something twinged in the last beatings of his physical body. He would never hold her again. Never see her again.

THURSDAY

NIGEL

"Is he asleep?"

"I think so."

He let them think so. Easier than finding the energy to squeeze her hand again. Another long pause. The crackle of the fire. The whisper of the sea and shifting sand. The last people on earth. Soon to be one less.

"A while ago you spoke to him about seeing god. You really believe these poor sick people see the creator of the universe coming for them in their final seconds?"

Uh-oh. Watch out, Singh.

"How can you deny it? It's universally reported. And don't give me that random-firing of neurons in the visual cortex bullshit!"

"Could you possibly adopt a neutral stance – just for a minute?"

Fat chance.

"I'm capable."

Uh-huh.

"All right, then. The dying person has sinned."

"How do you know that?"

"Correct me if I'm wrong, but aren't we all sinners in the eyes of god?"

"Well, yes…"

I don't need god for that, Nigel thought. I'm a sinner in my own eyes. Your brother and his family, Singh… if only I'd kept better guard on that data.

He pulled further into himself as they talked.

"I mean it's right there in your own New Testament. When Jesus said, 'Let he who is without sin cast the first stone,' he didn't expect to see any rocks flying. Montaigne said something to the effect that no man is so good that if all his actions were scrutinized he wouldn't deserve hanging ten times over."

"I prefer Jesus."

"I prefer Montaigne."

Abby gave his hand a gentle squeeze. "So would Nigel, I'm sure."

Right on, gorgeous girl.

"So however you look at it, the dying plague victims are in need of redemption and have been told to expect the divine. The hypoxia creates a self-fulfilling prophecy: They see the source of their redemption."

"Yes. God. He is the only source of redemption, so that's Who they see – that's Who is *there*. Otherwise nothing makes sense."

What will I see? Nigel thought. Empty space, right? That's the redemption I'm expecting.

Singh sighed. "I keep a quote from Mark Twain over my desk: *'It's no wonder that truth is stranger than fiction. Fiction has to make sense.'* Twain was talking about writing, but it applies to everything. Reality is under no obligation to make sense to us. It is what it is. It's up to us to make sense of it… if we wish. Too often we *don't* wish. Rather than probe reality, we simply concoct explanations. I call it explanation without investigation."

"Science has millions of unanswered questions."

Knew that one was coming.

"Of course. That doesn't stop us from asking them, however. But see, unanswered questions make people uncomfortable. The human mind craves order and symmetry. Order and symmetry demand that when something happens – good or bad – it shouldn't simply *happen*, it should happen for a *reason*… it should have a *purpose*. We find comfort in that. So we search for the reason, and if we can't find one, do we say, 'Sorry, I just don't know?' That's the honest answer. But no, we fill in the blank with what best fits our worldview. And that's where the trouble begins."

"Trouble as in God, you mean?"

Nigel could hear the acid in her tone.

"Well, what greater source of order and symmetry can you imagine than a Supreme Being? But we also fill the blanks with Satan, demons, aliens... take your pick."

Abby's brief laugh carried a derisive edge. "Aliens... really."

"Let's take demons then. A medieval mother says, 'My daughter wouldn't act that way. This isn't like her at all. She must be possessed! Call the priest!' As soon as the words 'She must be possessed!' pass the mother's lips, she finds a sort of comfort amid her terror. That makes sense to her. And not only does that offer a cause, it offers a solution: 'Call the priest!'"

"The Church has had many successful exorcisms."

"Has it? I'll have to take your word for it. But the same mindset carries over to this plague. Humanity is being wiped out, or very nearly so. Everyone asks, Why? No one wants to hear that it's happened to countless species through time. People think of dinosaurs and dodos, but three species go extinct every hour of every day. So why not *Homo sapiens*? As to *why*? Because shit happens. But no one wants to hear that, and I mean *no one* – neither the rational nor the irrational folks. Some*one* or some*thing* caused this. If it isn't God's will then it's an alien virus or human hubris."

"God made us in His image and we let Him down. He's cleaning house, as He did with the Flood."

She's a tough one, Singh. Lovable but unshakable in her faith. Quit while you're ahead – while you've still got *a head.*

"See what you've done there?" Singh said with a good-natured laugh. "You've tied up the whole situation in a neat little package: God made us, he owns us, and he's simply performing a periodic winnowing. Everything explained. I can stop thinking now."

"Better than 'Shit happens,' I'll tell you that."

Abby was always a good counterpuncher. But behind all that Nigel sensed a growing rapport between the two of them. Not affection, but a connection. Singh seemed a decent sort. Hadn't he found an ambulance to bring them here? Under different circumstances Nigel might be jealous, but he was glad Abby wouldn't be alone when he… left. And Singh was doing a good job of keeping her from going all God-Squaddy. He was good for her.

I was good for her too. Wasn't I? I must have been good for something other than chasing down other people's miseries for news.

"But shit *does* happen," Singh said. "Take lung cancer. Easily ninety percent of cases are due to smoking. That's a comforting symmetry to non-smokers: 'Oh well, he smoked; that won't happen to me.' Most of the remaining cancers are due to radon or asbestos or some other environmental factor. But what of the little old lady living a clean life out in the country who develops a primary lung tumor? Shit happens – shit, in this case, being a spontaneous mutation from unrepaired replication errors or random molecular events. It could have been other shit, like abnormal cell division or transposons and such, but let's just stick with a spontaneous mutation. That first plague fly was a spontaneous mutation: Shit happened."

"How do you know that?"

Good question.

"My brother told me. He was an expert on insect mutations."

"Maybe it wasn't so 'spontaneous.' Maybe God caused that mutation and–"

Nigel heard himself half groan, half sigh as he slipped another notch – the next-to-last notch.

Abby's grip tightened on his hand. He could feel her warm breath on his face as she leaned over him.

"Nigel! Nigel, what's wrong?"

You're kidding, right? You know perfectly well what's wrong. This is it. The last ride. The big adventure.

I'm scared, Abby.

I'm scared. Make it stop.

And then light, pale yellow, diffuse, as if seen through fogged glass, grew in his vision.

"Is the sun rising?" He could barely hear his own voice.

"Soon, honey. Soon, but not yet."

"I see light."

"The light!" Her hand crushed his fingers. He didn't mind. "What else, Nigel? What else?"

Something moving in the light…

A semi-translucent figure approached through the glow – small, with an unsteady gait. The closer it came, the sharper its features until he recognized…

Bandora.

Nigel might have laughed if the little guy hadn't been holding a beige capsule. He heard a faceless priest's words echo from his Catholic boyhood: *Take and eat, for this is my body.*

That unholy communion still haunted him

And then he remembered Singh's words from minutes or hours ago: *They see the source of their redemption…*

Is that what I'm seeing?

"Nigel?" Abby's voice echoed from far away as Bandora began to fade with the light. "What do you see?"

Bandora dissolved. Smoke. Unreal. A figment. Hypoxia…

Only formless gray now. The void opening as everything shut down.

No God. Just nothing.

Poor Abby…

Poor Nigel.

I'm scared. I don't want to go.

"I see…"

Nothing.

No. Don't be that man. Not in this last moment. The only moment left. Let her think you're saved. A vital lie…

Summoning the last of his strength, he took as deep a breath as he could and stretched his face into a smile. "I see Him, Abs… all white light and shining… too bright to look at… going home…"

And then the gray closed in for good.

ABBY

"Nigel?" Abby shook him, gently. "Nigel, don't go. Please, don't go!"

He couldn't go, couldn't be gone. Not Nigel. She'd known he was dying but she'd never accepted that he'd *die*. She thought she'd prepared herself for it but she hadn't. She looked up, her eyes blurring with tears that burned right down to her heart. On the other side of the dunes the sky was turning red with a new day but Nigel was gone and what good was a new day without Nigel?

She sobbed and felt ready to fly apart. She wanted to run into the sea and let it consume her. It wasn't supposed to be this way.

Going home. That's what he'd said. She looked up at the red sky. He'd seen God. Even for all Nigel's sins and his raging against her belief, He had come for him. God had chosen to take Nigel and leave her. She could cry. She could grieve. But she could not doubt her Lord.

Nigel was saved.

She closed her eyes, and in the first warm rays of the sun, she tilted her head back and sent up a silent prayer of thanks and love.

When she finally looked round, she saw Singh, kneeling beside Nigel, his face wet with tears.

"After what you told me about him," he said softly, "he must have loved you very much."

"We loved each other more than we knew, I think. Certainly more than we let on." The terrible truth of those words pierced her. "But you barely knew him."

"I researched him, I've been following him. I knew him well enough to appreciate his dying words."

Abby had too big a hole in her life right now to wonder what he was talking about. Nigel… her Nigel was gone.

———————

They buried Nigel on the beach he loved.

Gan – he'd asked her to call him Gan – found a folding shovel in a compartment of the ambulance and dug the grave. After Nigel was covered and rocks placed to mark the spot, Abby prayed over him while Gan stood silently by. When she was done, she forced herself to turn away and start back up the dune. Near the top she turned and saw Gan squatting beside the grave. He pressed a hand into the pile of sand and left a deep print.

"Why did you do that?"

Did it have a meaning? Some Hindu thing?

"He was a good man."

"Why do you say that? I wouldn't think that you… after your family…"

"It became clear to me in his last moments."

"I don't understand."

"I know." As she turned away and continued up the dune she thought she heard him whisper, "I doubt you ever will."

ABBY

Funny, she thought, realizing it wasn't very funny at all, that she and Nigel had always fantasized about living together in a house in Sandbanks. Their holidays in Poole were always in bed and breakfasts or small hotels, but they'd drive along the row of sea-front mansions and laugh – back in the days when they laughed a lot – as they decided which one they liked best, which one was too tacky, and how life was going to be when they were part of that exclusive club of homeowners.

It would never happen of course. The houses in Sandbanks cost upward of seven or eight million. Even if Nigel had written the novel he'd never really got round to starting, they would have to have been the luckiest couple in the world to make enough to buy a dream house. And anyway, the dream had always been enough. The small fantasy. The drive and the shared wishing, and then back into Poole for dinner and sex with the sea air still in their hair.

Now, in a way, they had become kind of a Sandbanks couple. Not like they'd dreamed, but still…

She'd chosen a house – a mansion – with huge ceiling-to-floor windows where she could look out and see the beach where he was buried whenever she needed too, even in winter when it eventually came. The original owners were nowhere to be seen – a smart stylish couple in their forties, judging by the photographs and sailing clothes in the cupboards – and she figured they wouldn't be coming back.

Most of the houses were empty. This one wouldn't be though. She would make this her home. The air was clean, no dead bodies lying in the streets, and Nigel was near her. Why would she want to be anywhere else?

After they'd buried Nigel, she felt an awkwardness with Gan, as if the thin thread that connected them had been broken, which in a way it had. They were strangers brought together by the world crumbling around them, and now that Nigel was dead, it felt like the morning after a one-night stand where something so intimate had been shared and then a new day dawned and you had nothing to say to each other.

She'd told him she was going to stay here – close to her husband. He had nodded and said that he would likely move on. He had no wife to get back to even before the plague – his life had been a quiet one: his work, his patients and occasional visits to his brother's family. He had liked it that way. She had nodded and scrambled up the sandy steps to the mile-long stretch of mansions and begun her search for one to live in.

"Get away from here!" came from one – a sickly scream, but whoever was inside still managed to launch a bottle from the window. Abby hadn't noticed Gan following her until he grabbed her and pulled her back from the missile's path.

At first he'd said he'd stay until she was settled. He took the ambulance on several trips into Poole and loaded it with supplies. He was vague about where he'd found everything. Left behind by dead hoarders, she guessed.

He found a generator. Fuel. Food. Medicines. Cases and cases of bottled water. Wine too. The house was big enough to store it all. He also brought two shotguns and boxes of shells.

She wondered why he'd brought two. She could only fire one, and he'd insisted he was leaving.

Three days later he was still here.

They sat out on the beautiful verandah and stared out over the sea. Abby had cooked them a spaghetti dinner and between them they'd drunk a bottle of good red wine. The air was still warm and the sea sang to them in the silent world.

"Can I stay?" Gan asked, eventually. "I don't want to live alone."

"But you told me you've always lived alone."

"When I was surrounded by a city full of people, I preferred alone. Now when they're all gone…" He shrugged.

Somehow, she understood.

"Sure. There's no shortage of rooms, that's for sure."

She didn't look at him but down at the beach where the sand shifted in the breeze. The rocks marking Nigel's grave stayed firm. She'd be happy to have Gan around. Abby was not a loner and the world was too empty now for two people who knew each other to walk in different directions. She sipped her wine and quietly mourned her husband. The sky was finally darkening into midnight blue when Gan spoke again.

"Did you ever hear of the Toba catastrophe?"

Soft. Melodic. He had a beautiful speaking voice, she realized.

"No. What was it?"

'A volcano erupted in Indonesia some 75,000 years ago."

She smiled at him. "How old do you think I am?"

The wine buzzed in her blood. Despite everything, she felt okay. Maybe not fine – maybe she wouldn't be fine for a long time – but okay.

"Very funny. But it's relevant." He rested his feet on the top bar of the sleek steel verandah railings and leant back in his chair. "You see, it didn't just erupt – it *super*erupted, throwing so much debris into the air that a volcanic winter followed, triggering the last ice age. Do you know how long that ice age lasted?"

Abby shook her head, listening.

"Ten thousand years, although it was the ash fall that proved lethal to most of humanity. At the end of the dying from the volcanic winter and the ash, the number of human survivors in the whole *world* equaled the population of pre-plague Glastonbury. Fewer than ten thousand mating pairs."

"Good God!" Abby turned away from the beach – from Nigel – and stared.

"I don't know about 'good,' but the event caused a genetic bottleneck that changed humanity forever. We were a much more diverse species before the catastrophe."

"And you're saying we're facing another of those now?"

She hadn't asked him about the population in Poole when he'd fetched their supplies, but he hadn't mentioned meeting anyone and she'd understood what that meant. The plague had gripped England and the rest of the world and wasn't letting go. The TV had given up even pretending to broadcast and the only thing on the radio was a pre-recorded message telling people to stay inside away from the flies.

"I've no doubt of it. Peoples like the Inuit will probably remain unaffected, because no flies will be wandering above the Arctic Circle.

I suppose a certain number of refugees will flee north, but the rest of humanity… we're witnessing a kind of species entropy, the birth pangs of a different human race, a genetic change so profound that I can't blame anyone who imagines the hand of god in it."

"Of course, you had to say 'imagine,' didn't you."

He smiled. "Of course."

He reminded her of Nigel. Not on the outside, of course, but they were certainly intellectual bedfellows, although Gan was gentler in his approach to her beliefs. Similar but different. If only two people were to remain in this corner of Armageddon then there could be worse pairings.

Pairings…she flushed slightly at the realization that her thought had mirrored his words.

Mating pairs.

Certainly he didn't expect them to…no, she couldn't see that happening.

But company…company would be nice.

THE AUTHORS

Sarah Pinborough is a critically acclaimed award-winning author of horror, crime and YA fiction. She has also written for 'New Tricks' on the BBC, and has a horror film and an original TV series in development. She lives in London.

F. Paul Wilson is an award-winning, NY Times bestselling author of over 50 novels in many genres and numerous short stories translated into twenty-four languages. He is best known as creator of the urban mercenary Repairman Jack.

www.shadowridgepress.com

Printed in Great Britain
by Amazon